He was just straightening when the blast of a heavy-caliber rifle threatened to jar his eyeteeth loose. The stallion dropped, twitched a couple of times, and was still.

Now they were close in and, despite the darkness, Rudge could see shadowy figures on equally indistinct horses. . . .

Seconds later he felt warm blood trickling into his eyes. He lay half sprawled over the downed stallion and its warmth brought him back to full awareness. He was sure he'd taken one of them out of action but the second stranger was still out there somewhere. He wiped the blood from his eyes and prayed his vision might still be good. Cautiously, he tried his legs. Everything seemed to work. For everything to *continue* working he had to see the other man first. . .

J.B. Masterson is a longtime California rancher. This is his first novel.

RUDGE

J. B. MASTERSON

CHARTER
NEW YORK

A Division of Charter Communications Inc.
A GROSSET & DUNLAP COMPANY
51 Madison Avenue
New York, New York 10010

RUDGE

An ACE CHARTER Book
Published by arrangement with Doubleday & Company, Inc.

Published simultaneously in Canada

Manufactured in the United States of America
2 4 6 8 0 9 7 5 3 1

I

"What's the matter, Limey, gettin' too hot for you?"

Rudge finished removing his coat and hung it carefully over the back of his chair. Turning back to the other man, he said, "So hot that perhaps it would be preferable if we were all to take off our coats." He rolled his shirt sleeves up past his elbows and stood beside the chair.

The thin one, called Doc, merely smiled.

The beefy man turned a dull red. "You sayin' I'm cheatin'?"

"No such thing," Rudge said, and finished rolling up his sleeves.

The third man said nothing. Rudge stood beside his chair and waited. Silence settled over the sparse afternoon crowd. It was broken only when the thin one—Doc—widened his smile and stood to remove his frock coat. "Sure is gettin' hot in here," he agreed.

Still Rudge waited. The beefy one and the silent third man glanced at odd-looking Colts strapped low around Rudge's waist. They got to their feet and began taking off their coats.

After that the cards ran almost as well for Rudge as they had an hour ago when the strangers had offered to teach him this outlandish American game called poker.

The silent man surveyed his cards disgustedly. "Tapioca," he growled and tossed in his hand. It was the first time he had spoken. None of the onlookers volunteered to take his place as he left the table. Despite having taken his coat off, the beefy, red-faced man was now sweating profusely. The deal came to Rudge again. He rolled his sleeves a turn higher and handled the cards with an exaggerated and careful slowness, realizing suddenly that his luck had turned entirely too good.

So that was why the thin one was smiling. Doc knew he'd been caught cheating, but now, by deliberately making Rudge win too often, he hoped to shift the blame. Rudge won another hand. He won two more hands before he managed to shift the deal back to Doc. When Doc dealt, Rudge won again.

"I really don't need your help," Rudge said.

The onlookers were puzzled but Doc was not. Still smiling, holding his cards close to his vest, he abruptly threw them down on the table. From behind the fanned cards Doc had produced a Deringer.

Rudge shot from under the table. The gambler was blown backward out of his chair. Rudge stood, holstering an odd-looking Colt. "Does anyone wish to suggest this was not cricket?" Then he remembered he was no longer in a country where boys played at that game. "A fair and legitimate self-defense?" he amended.

Nobody did. The beefy man sat rigid, both hands on the table. His complexion was no longer red. Rudge scooped in the pot, flicked out a double eagle, and pocketed the rest. "Is twenty dollars sufficient to bury the man who deals from the middle?"

Nobody seemed inclined to haggle.

Rudge picked up his swallowtail coat and for a split second considered putting it on. But he had observed during that Mexican adventure that even bullfighters never needlessly tempt a beast. Coat over his arm, he moved carefully toward the street. He thought he had made it when the shooting started. It came from the back door.

The silent man who had been tapped out earlier, he guessed. But now other guns were popping. Rudge drew both Colts and fired toward the rear door. There was a shrill, almost feminine shriek and abruptly the shooting was over. In the sudden calm Rudge had time to cross the wooden walkway and unhitch his gray. He rode his horse at a gallop a quarter of a mile until the last house of the single-street town was behind him. Finally, satisfied that nobody was following, he slowed the gray studhorse to a trot.

He had gotten away with his life and something over a thousand dollars. Rudge fancied he ought to be happy. He patted his saddlebags and congratulated himself on having stocked up with provender before going into the Golden Eagle for a final drink. It hadn't been much of a town any-way, he sour-graped. But somewhere, someday, Joseph Bentley Rudge knew he had to settle down. He had just blown another chance in Soda Springs, Territory of New Mexico.

The road led gradually upward until by nightfall the *saguaro-* and *cholla*-dotted plain around the town had yielded to scrubby juniper, whose purple berries the gray rejected after a single sniff. Rudge, who had tasted those berries in London, wished momentarily he were back where he had first sampled gin. But he owed England nothing. Not since 1865. He glanced behind.

For a couple of miles the trail was visible before it disap-peared amid low, clumping junipers. Here and there hum-mocks of coarse grass sprang up in between. Not enough for the gray. He weighed the discomforts of a dry camp against the greater annoyance of a rattler-struck horse and decided to make a night of it.

The gray was not a desert horse and had never mastered the trick of drinking from a canteen, but Rudge knew that, unless he wanted to walk, the horse's thirst was more im-portant than his own. He emptied one of his canvas water bags into his hat and the stallion did the best he could.

Rudge's black, unyieldingly flat-brimmed, flat-crowned, and tapered hat merited better treatment but the gold pan was too shallow to water a horse. He supposed he ought to

get a more inconspicuous hat—one that would make him
look less like an errant Spaniard, but with his jet hair and
mustache it was sometimes advantageous in these countries
to be taken for something other than English. When the
horse finished drinking from his *sevillano* Rudge shook it
dry and put it back on. He hobbled the horse and stretched
his snake rope in a circle before settling down in the middle
with his blanket. He inspected his Colts before the light was
all gone, then tried to compose himself to sleep until moon-
rise. It was the gray's snort that woke him.

There was always the chance that whoever traveled in
total darkness along this road was a law-abiding citizen in
pursuit of his own legitimate business. But the odds against
it were likely enough for Rudge to draw on his boots and
buckle his Colts hurriedly. The darkness was as absolute as
the silence. He listened, caught the faint skittering of a kan-
garoo rat, wondered if that other sound was the movement
of a snake, and then he heard the distant creak of saddle
leather. He hunkered down amid the junipers and waited to
see if the stranger would pass.

There were two of them. The road, he reminded himself,
did lead to another settlement high in the mountains.
Strangers had as much right to use it as he did. But Rudge
was not hungry for company at this moment. He decided to
ooze over toward the studhorse and grasp his lips lest the
gray be more eager for companionship. He was just
straightening when the blast of a heavy-caliber rifle threatened to jar his eyeteeth loose. The stallion dropped,
twitched a couple of times, and was still.

But now they were close in, and despite the darkness,
Rudge could see shadowy figures on equally indistinct
horses. He fired and the leader fell backward to slide un-
gracefully off the rump of his mount. The man behind fired.
At that instant Rudge's stallion gave a final twitch and
spoiled his aim. For the tiniest of instants Rudge saw the

blaze of broad daylight, then it dissolved into shooting stars that faded once more into blackness.

Seconds later he felt warm blood trickling into his eyes. He lay half-sprawled over the downed stallion and its warmth brought him back to full awareness. He was sure he'd taken one of them out of action but the second stranger was still out there somewhere. He wiped blood from his eyes and prayed his vision might still be good. Cautiously, he tried his legs. Everything seemed to work. For everything to *continue* working he had to see the other man first.

The hills on the opposite side of the immense basin were rimmed with a halo of light that seemed to shimmer. Somewhere far behind him a coyote began a shrill protest at this outrage. Rudge blinked and wiped his eyes again. The coyote had been taken in by the moon's old trick of rising unpredictably. So had Rudge. In minutes that orb would clear the hill and the whole country would be lit up well enough to sight a rifle.

He wanted to feel the burning crease on the top of his head, put a handkerchief over it to stanch this blinding and bloody annoyance. But someone might be watching, waiting for a dead man to move. He heard a horse blow behind him. From the corner of his eye he saw a riderless mustang unconcernedly picking at the sparse grass among the junipers. With nightfall their pungent odor of London gin permeated the air.

The crease in his scalp had done nothing to fuddle his thinking. Rudge knew he had done more than the usual quota of things calculated to send hard-eyed strangers out looking for him; but those things had been done in other states—other countries. In any event, for the last two months he had led an exemplary life, passing swiftly through new country and leaving no trace or grudge behind him. Until this afternoon in the Golden Eagle.

Somewhere behind him Rudge heard the faint rustle of grass as the last of the cardsharpers moved. Logic told him the man couldn't see him or there would have been a more accurate shot by now. The horse whinnied at the smell of blood. Rudge began a slow-as-molasses ooze down off his still-warm stallion, praying he would make no noise.

His prayer was not answered. A twig snapped beneath him. Rudge transmuted his slow slide into a frantic scramble just as the rifle barked and another bullet plowed into the dead stallion.

He bracketed the rifle's flash with twin Colts and in the echoing aftermath of the shots he heard the clatter of a rifle hitting the ground. He crouched a long time behind the horse. Finally he holstered the Colts and began dabbing at his head with a handkerchief.

By now the bleeding had nearly stopped. He was tempted to wet his handkerchief from the remaining water bag, but he knew he might have better uses for the water before he reached the next oasis fifty miles and seven thousand feet away.

The moon was fully risen by now. The strangers' horses had gotten over their nervousness and stood quietly a hundred yards off, cropping at sparse clumps of *zacatón* between the junipers. Local horses, Rudge guessed. His huge gray had disdained the coarse desert saw grass.

He knew he had hit both men. But were they dead? The second man had only been hit because he had been negligent in his investigation of Rudge's death. Rudge did not want the compliment returned. He closed his eyes and held his breath, straining to hear the slightest breathing. A hundred yards away the horses were puffing like steam engines, jangling bridles and snagging stirrups in the scrub juniper. He waited for them to stop but the horses were uninterested in Rudge's problems.

He found his stiff black *sevillano*. Holed squarely through the tapered crown. It was a trick that probably antedated Greek experiments with wooden horses, but it was the only thing he could devise with the materials at hand. He held up the hat with the barrel of one Colt. There was no reaction. He lobbed a rock well beyond where he had seen the rifle flash. Still nothing apart from a pricking of horses' ears.

By now the moon was well up. Instead of sticking his head up over the dead studhorse, he crawled as noiselessly as he could some distance to one side of the still-warm barricade and cautiously raised his head. And saw the other man. From the acute discomfort of the angle at which the man lay, Rudge knew the man with the rifle was not faking it. Still, he crawled closer and waited a full minute for some twitch or blink. Finally he decided one of the pair of shysters was no longer dangerous.

So where was the other one? He was almost tempted to stand up. But Rudge had not made it to thirty-five by pretending to be braver than he was. He considered the fallen rifle and decided against it, knowing any further action would be in range of the twin Colts so skillfully altered by a London gunsmith.

He crawled in what he thought was the right direction but there was no corpse. The moon was making it nearly as bright as day now. The gamblers must've both been still on the trail when they shot his gray. If he kept on crawling through the juniper scrub this way, sooner or later he was going to meet up with a rattler He took a deep breath, commended his soul to the properly delegated authorities, and raised his head for a quick look around.

The man he had blown off the horse had crawled a few feet. Rudge felt the man's wrist and knew he would not crawl any farther. He reloaded his Colts and thought about catching the horses. Then he realized there was something odd. He studied the dead man. The first man he had looked at was the beefy one who had tried to outbluff him. With Doc shot in the saloon, that accounted for two of the gamblers. But this one . . . was not the taciturn man who had muttered "Tapioca," and pulled out of the game. Rudge had never seen this pimpled, boyish face before. Didn't look a day over seventeen. And now he would never grow old. Rudge sighed and went off to catch the horses.

As horses not uncommonly do, these kept just beyond grabbing distance, dragging reins as they ambled leisurely through the junipers. Rudge wondered if they could be lured by offering water. Then he remembered that his *sevillano* would no longer hold water.

He picked up one of the dead men's hats and saw it was also holed. Not a fresh bullet hole; this low-crowned Stetson was so worn it had parted at the crease. The other hat was loose-woven plowboy straw. Rudge was about to give up when he realized that the smell of water and the sound of a gurgling canteen ought to be enough. He went back to the dead gray and searched for his other, still unused, water bag. He sighed again. The horse had fallen on the bag and his weight had popped out the corncob plug. Rudge faced fifty uphill miles without a drop of water.

There was only one thing to do if he wanted to continue living. He had to go back to Soda Springs and pick up more water and a fresh outfit. He had to catch one of those horses.

It turned out easier than he had expected because at a crucial moment one horse flung its head and the dragging reins fouled on a juniper.

It couldn't be more than ten or twelve miles back to town. Start now and maybe he could get there and headed back out of town before the sun turned this basin into a brazier. Then Rudge knew that in a town as small as Soda Springs somebody was sure to know who these horses belonged to. There was only one way to avoid tiresome explanations. He mounted the wiry pinto he had caught and chased the other horse. Twenty minutes later he had lashed the two bodies across the extra horse's back and was clopping back down the trail toward Soda Springs, Terr. of N. Mex.

II

It was dawning as Rudge entered Soda Springs. But the inhabitants knew what the sun would be like in another hour, so a surprising number of them were already well into their morning chores, swamping out the livery stable, doing the same for the saloon and dance hall.

The balding, sleeve-gartered proprietor of the Mercantile was sprinkling the boardwalk in front of his store with his thumb over a bottle that had once contained Green River but now held the alkaline and slightly purgative water that gave the town its name. He was reaching for a broom when his casual glance at the stranger riding into town with two horses caused the Mercantile owner to drop the bottle.

Rudge supposed he ought to have wrapped them in a tarp or blanket. But he had none to spare, and even if he'd had one he saw no profit in soiling it with leaky bodies. Besides, the townspeople would have to find out sooner or later. He rode as tall and straight as a cavalryman on parade, reins in his left hand and his right resting easily on his hip above the butt of one Colt.

One by one the early risers recognized the nature of his packhorse's burden. One by one each disappeared with an abruptness that reminded Rudge of his mother's cuckoo clock.

How much of Soda Springs's single street could he traverse before one of those cuckoo clocks would pop open again with a repeating rifle? It was, like any other game, a question of odds. Odds were that the citizens he was returning to this town were no more loved than the gamblers and misfits of any other town.

But one of them was still a boy. How much dislike could a boy accumulate in seventeen years? For an instant he almost laughed as he remembered a beardless host who had managed, in the last year of the war, to accumulate more grudges than most men could handle in a lifetime. But he suspected that even if the citizens of Soda Springs would not be outraged over killing a boy, they might draw the line at a smile. Killing, to be acceptable, must always be accompanied by a sanctimonious solemnity.

Somebody was scooting along the store fronts, half bent over as he ducked from pillar to sacked oats to rain barrel. Now what optimist had fitted his roof with gutters and rain barrel in this country? Rudge rode without changing position, his right hand still resting on his hip within comfortable distance of one altered Colt.

The figure who paralleled his progress down the street was too slight to be a man. Whatever the boy was up to, he was not trying to conceal himself. Rudge guessed he shouldn't have returned to town in just this fashion. He had been trying not to leave a trail. But events just would not leave him alone.

Even if he hadn't been forced to return to Soda Springs for water, it was necessary to demonstrate that the Limey was not to be followed and annoyed. Otherwise, he could have scalped them and let the Apaches claim the credit. *And ridden into the next town on two dead men's horses?*

His mind was wandering. It worried Rudge. He had seen it happen before. After a while men grew so tired of killing that the mistake they finally made often seemed deliberate. He had wondered if they came to believe they led charmed lives, that nothing could touch them—or if they no longer cared.

Rudge cared. From the corner of his eye he noted that the boy who followed him carried no gun. Unlike the others, this boy was not trying to pretend he did not see Rudge and the burden on his packhorse. Rudge wondered if there was any other less flamboyant way he could have returned. None, he decided. If he was going to ride a dead man's horse, it was best that there be no ambiguity over how that man had died.

A man before the swinging doors of the Golden Eagle studied Rudge's load unblinkingly, disdaining cuckoo-clock maneuvers as that boyish shadow oozed around him. Rudge sensed from the speculative stare that there would be no danger from that quarter. Any trouble would come from one of those disappearers. What was the boy up to, scooting along the street that way, trying to get himself killed? Rudge hoped he would not be inconvenienced by someone's ambition to be a hero. Even more, he hoped he could find the sheriff without having to ride the entire length of this single-street town.

When he saw it, the sheriff's office was a small building shoehorned between a tailor's and a saddlery. Bits of adobe were visible through a missing plank in the false front. The boy had stopped following him several doors short of the sheriff's. Rudge sighed and dismounted. He tied the horses to the rail and entered the open doorway.

When the ageing man behind the desk looked up in surprise Rudge knew that he was not surprised at all. Some cuckoo had ducked out of the back door of his clock and hot-footed it down here faster than Rudge had cared to push tired horses.

"Yes?" the sheriff asked. "Something I can do for you?"

"It's possible," Rudge said. "Do you know either of them?" He gestured out the door at the laden packhorse.

Citizens were appearing now that Rudge had tied up in front of the forces of righteousness. The graying, walrus-mustached sheriff scooted from behind the desk, moving faster than Rudge would have expected. He went to the hitching rack and shooed several boys away from the pack-horse. He turned to Rudge. "Yup. I know them."

"What sort of people were they?"

"Your kind."

Rudge studied the sheriff for a moment. "I do not assault innocent travelers in their sleep," he said pointedly. "Nor am I in the habit of shooting other people's horses. Now shall we discuss morality or legality?"

"Neither one," the sheriff said tiredly. "I don't give two hoots in hell how many of you tinhorns kill each other off. It's only when you bring down innocent bystanders that I get my dander up."

Rudge had not expected this. "Are you charging me with something?"

"Nope," the sheriff said. "That gray you rode out of town was worth about two of them mustangs. I reckon you come out even." He surveyed the corpses on the packhorse and spat tobacco. "Looks like Soda Springs come out about even too."

A man and a boy emerged from beneath the Fine Furniture and Funerals sign across the street, carrying a litter. The sheriff nodded and they undid the lashings. The corpses had stiffened into horseshoe attitudes and did not fit gracefully onto the litter. The man and boy got them both out of sight while the sheriff once more shooed clustering children.

The sheriff faced Rudge again. "Well?" he demanded.

"Exactly," Rudge said.

There was another silence while the sheriff's unblinking eyes took in Rudge's roady claw-hammer coat, the tall leanness of weathered skin still white enough to make his hair and mustache seem even blacker. "I've lost a day," Rudge finally hinted.

The sheriff did not reply.

"Any statements or depositions?"

"Nope. Town won't miss them *or* you. Long's I never see

your shadow 'round here again I reckon everything's settled."

It had been some time since anyone had spoken in this fashion to Rudge. He knew he ought to let well enough alone but the sheriff's attitude annoyed him. "I wonder," Rudge mused.

"Wonder what?"

"If everything's settled."

"Oh, they got friends," the sheriff reassured him. "Hang around long enough and you'll get yours."

"That's not what I was wondering." Rudge knew he ought to keep his mouth shut. Let it go. But this graying, walrus-mustached man was annoying Rudge far more than he could admit even to himself. "Your attitude seems cavalier even for this benighted territory," Rudge said. "Since you choose to prejudge a total stranger, perhaps you'll afford me the same opportunity?"

"Go ahead."

"I assume that I'm free to go. You realize, of course, that I would never have wasted time returning had it not been for a need of the water and supplies these ruffians destroyed. I'll not be leaving until I've replenished my kit. In the course of this act I shall undoubtedly exchange remarks with other citizens. Is there something you'd prefer to tell me at this time?"

"Can't think of anything."

"Oh?" Rudge tipped his hat and began untying the horses. *Let it go. Ignore a bitter old man. Get out of here!* But he could not suppress the little thrill of exultation that surged through him when the graying old man took the bait.

"Just what're you gettin' at, Limey?" the sheriff asked.

"You call me a tinhorn. Since you ascribe the name, should I not have the game?"

"Quit talkin' in circles."

"Extraordinary how eager you are to see the last of me.

Almost as if there were something you didn't wish me to discover."

The sheriff's eyes narrowed. "Just what is it you want?"

"The reward."

From the sheriff's look of blank surprise Rudge immediately knew two things: that he should have kept his mouth shut, and that there was no reward. The sheriff pitched his voice low enough not to be overheard. "You soapy son of a bitch," he promised, "in one hour the citizens of this town are gonna have their minds changed and decide on a necktie party. Now you git your water and git out!"

Rudge got on his horse. He tipped his hat to the sheriff and led his packhorse back up the single street to the Mercantile.

The balding proprietor did not once look squarely at Rudge. He looked slightly beyond, as if expecting someone to come storming into the store behind him. Rudge made his purchases as expeditiously as possible. He had already outfitted once. But this time he would be traveling with two horses and it remained to be seen whether these local beasts would move better or worse than his gray. And he now had another thousand dollars he had not possessed the first time he had fitted out to leave Soda Springs. He bought a bottle of Green River. He was heading for the door with one armful of small packages when it finally occurred to Rudge to ask, "Would you say your sheriff was an honest man?"

The Mercantile's owner goggled for a moment. "Mr. Jason fought for the Union," he sputtered.

So, to Rudge's knowledge, had a great many scoundrels. But he supposed the remark was meant for a recommendation. This time he managed to restrain himself. But as he turned to step outside he could not refrain from a small smile. To insult scoundrels was a pointless pursuit. But if the sheriff was an honorable man then he would appreciate the depth of the insult he had offered and had returned. *And damn all the smug sons of bitches!* Still half smiling, he stepped out into the sunshine.

"Mr. Rudge!"

The slight-bodied man moved so quickly that it took all of Rudge's self-control not to drop his packages and whip out his Colts. Then as his eyes adjusted to sunlight outside the store he had an instant to reflect on what the sheriff had said. He had come dangerously close to shooting a boy who couldn't be much older than the pimply-faced one of the pair he had already shot. "Yes," Rudge said. "What is it?"

"I been holdin' your horses for you."

"The hitching rack was serving that purpose most admirably," Rudge snapped. This was the boy who had paralleled his progress down the street to the sheriff's. He gave the street a quick inspection and began stowing his purchases about the packhorse. So far, it seemed, the sheriff had done nothing to stir up the town. Rudge wondered which of them was misjudging the other.

He finished stowing and the boy was still there. Rudge was annoyed at this transparent extortion but he didn't want still another confrontation. He tossed two bits.

"No, sir." The boy handed the money back.

Rudge was in the saddle now. "Just what is it you want?"

"Let me go with you."

"Go with me? Where?"

"Out of here—anywhere!"

Oh, Jesus! At thirty-five Rudge had almost forgotten how he had been at this age—before his youthful restlessness had been cured by a couple of wars. "Now what on earth tempts you to throw in with me?"

"You killed Bus Harwood and Roan Gantwell. Saved me the trouble."

This was the first time Rudge had heard their names. He managed not to smile. This boy was going to turn out handsome someday—if he lived that long. The youth had his eyes on those twin altered Colts. Rudge sighed. "You undoubtedly have no family and in any event they mistreat you, never once appreciating the sterling qualities in your character?"

The boy's eyes widened. "Yeah!"

"And in appreciation of these slights you're prepared to hit the trail, efface yourself from their drab and wretched lives—returning only at the end of a brilliant career in some dangerous and adventure-filled profession."

The boy's mouth was open. Rudge glanced down the street at the sheriff's office and for an instant was tempted to give the town full measure. Then he remembered that the town had done him no injury. It was only the sanctimonious sheriff who had offered Rudge gratuitous insult. "Do you have your own gun and horse?" he asked.

The boy nodded.

"Saddle and full kit?"

This time the boy's nod was not quite so prompt. Which meant, Rudge guessed, that the boy knew where he could steal them. He took the two-bit piece back out of his pocket and tossed it. "An envelope and one sheet of paper," he said.

The boy was in and out of the Mercantile in a flash. Rudge pulled a deck of cards from an inside coattail pocket and scribbled a note on their flat surface. He sealed the envelope and handed it to the boy. "Deliver this to Sheriff Jason," he said. "Then you can saddle up and join me."

Joy unconfined. Then doubt entered the boy's mind. "Can't I come now?"

"First the note," Rudge said firmly. "You'll be riding a single horse. No reason why you can't catch up."

The boy nodded glumly and began walking toward the sheriff's. Rudge spurred his mustang and headed back out of town the way he had come in. It was nearly nine o'clock.

At least he had the sun on his back. It would be there without the slightest hint or hope of shade for the next four hours. He stopped in front of the livery stable long enough to fill canteens and water his horses. Nearing the edge of town he reflected, glum as the boy, that after four hours the sun would no longer be at his back. All afternoon he would ride straight into it.

Damn that smug sheriff! What right had he to be holier-than-thou? But as he rode back toward where he had bested those ruffians, Rudge knew the sheriff was not all wrong. What had happened to Joseph Bentley Rudge who had read law and seen a brilliant career before him?

A boy has the face he was born with. By forty a man has the face he deserves.

"*But I'm only thirty-five,*" Rudge thought.

"*Close enough,*" his recording angel replied.

"*But I'm not a tinhorn.*"

"*No,*" his recording angel conceded. "*You're worse.*"

"*But it was war. I was a patriot.*"

"*The last refuge of a scoundrel.*" Rudge's recording angel was quoting Dr. Johnson.

Still, it was sobering to know that at least some part of humanity was already reading his past on his face. It was time to settle down. Join the human race for better or for worse. Join while there was still some chance they would let him.

The mustang weighed several hundred less than his dead gray but this wiry beast seemed to enjoy the desert sun. And despite having borne two men into town already this morning, the packhorse plodded along without dragging back on the lead rope. Rudge glanced over his shoulder. The trail and town were both visible behind. There was no sign of the young hero worshiper who planned on joining him.

"*Wasn't one war enough?*"

"*Would have been if we'd won,*" Rudge replied.

"*Were you a patriot down there too?*"

Rudge sighed. He was losing these arguments with increasing frequency. "*But I did my good deed today,*" he insisted.

Back down in Soda Springs his good deed was fuming

over the choice of sweeping out the office and jail *versus* the sheriff's offer to tell his sister on him.

It was all so unfair. What kind of a horrible lie had Mr. Rudge written about him? It must be a real whopper. The boy had never seen the sheriff so mad before.

While Sheriff Jason kept one glowering eye on the boy, he smoothed out the crumpled note and once more read the neat copperplate script.

> *Sheriff: Please keep this citizen of your fair city suitably occupied until my corrupting influence has attained an appropriate distance.*
>
> > *May the right prevail!*
> >
> > *Jos. B. Rudge*

III

As he climbed out of the Soda Springs basin the smell of juniper was not so all-prevailing as it had been by moonlight, but even now the London gin stink lay light beneath a layer of heat. The mustangs ate up the slow miles and he found his gray. The coyotes had already been at the horse.

Rudge sighed and dismounted. He tied the mustangs and began sorting the usable from the spoilt in his scattered pack. Studying the dead gray, Rudge felt an unaccustomed moisture about his eyes. In spite of the sheriff's having acknowledged his *jure belli* rights, Rudge didn't think he had come out even. Two live mustangs and two dead men were no even trade for the magnificent gray that had carried him all the way from—

He heard the single echoless snap of a distant shot. Were the Indians up to mischief around here? Should have asked back in Soda Springs. He wiped his eyes and gave the killing ground a final look over. The mustangs began moving up the trail. He was already a thousand feet higher but the sun and temperature were climbing with each mile he rode.

Damn Soda Springs! If he'd had anything to do with cutting trail or settling this country Rudge would have found some way around that badwater sink. If he'd bypassed that hardluck town he might have been well on his way to San Francisco by now—happier and less aware of the changes time had wrought in a gentleman.

Pair of strangers might have been happier too. And he would still be riding the gray. This mustang was willing, but it was so small that he caught himself instinctively lifting his feet lest the beast walk out from under him.

Two more flat, echoless shots in the distance. He stood as high as the stirrups would let him and studied the country. Nothing but endless miles of junipers on this plain that tilted until one end was in hell and the other in snow. He sighed and urged the horses on.

Hours passed until the sun was in front of him, shining squarely in his eyes. He tilted his hat and tried not to think of all the cool and comfortable places he had been forced to leave. Then abruptly he broke out of his reverie with a sudden realization: he was not alone!

He would have been unable to explain how he knew it but the knowledge was there—that he, the mustangs, and the horned toads were not the only beings enduring this heat. He struggled not to show what he knew. If an Indian was going to bushwhack him, Rudge knew he was already dead. Keeping his hands from the altered Colts, he began a slow, carefully inconspicuous survey of the country. Before he had time to give up, the mustang's ears told him that whoever it was lay ahead.

He tightened his knees slightly and prepared to drop the reins. The packhorse tossed his head and jerked the lead. Rudge used the jostling to get his hands closer to his pistols. Then he saw the dead horse up ahead.

It was roan and nearly as large as his gray. It had not been long dead—unless somebody had gone to the trouble of puncturing gas pockets. He was within twenty paces of the dead animal when a rifle appeared over it. "Just hold it there, mister!"

Rudge held it. The rifle continued aiming at him but he could not get more than a glimpse of gray hair beyond it. Several seconds passed. "I've been shot at some already today," Rudge finally said. "Do you mind if I dismount?"

"Slow and easy makes for a long and happy life."

"That," Rudge said, "is an axiom of limited application.

Had I not been reasonably fast—" He left it to dangle along with the mustang's reins.

Another couple of inches of gray head appeared from behind the horse. "Sorry, stranger," the old man said. "Man tends to forget his company manners out here."

The old man's speech was American but there was a faint overlay of something not native to this continent. After a moment Rudge decided the man behind the dead horse must have spent some small part of his life in Scotland. Rudge realized abruptly that when his tired mustangs stopped moving it could be even hotter. He came around behind the dead horse. The man was anywhere from fifty to seventy—gray and shriveled from years of desert sun. He was hatless, which is inadvisable. He was bleeding from one shoulder, which is more so. "How far is the next shade?" Rudge asked.

"Thirty miles uphill and no doctor."

By Rudge's reckoning it must be about the same distance back to Soda Springs.

"'Tis," the old man agreed. "But it's downhill and they've a man there can dig out bullets."

Please God, not again! Rudge controlled himself. "Can you ride?"

"Won't know till I try."

Rudge studied the sky. It still lacked several hours for the sun to go down. He led his horses to stand where they contributed some shade while he undid the pack he had hung from a dead bushwhacker's roping saddle. When he uncorked a water bag the old man took a cautious swallow and coughed. His face turned a shade paler and his shoulder oozed blood. After a moment he pulled himself together. "Have to chaw it a bit afore ye swallow," he said, "but if you're thirsty enough, Soda Springs water tastes pretty good."

"I doubt if they'll ever have a brewery," Rudge said as he began lashing his outfit in the tarp. He was going to have to pile boulders over it to keep the coyotes out. The old man took another sip and this time the water stayed with him. "Was it Indians?" Rudge asked.

The old man gave him an odd look. "I'm Maclendon," he finally said.

And I'm non sequitur, Rudge thought, but he limited himself to a nod.

"Stranger here?" the old man asked.

"I'm rapidly learning the customs of the country."

"People here know I always got on well enough with the Indians," Maclendon explained.

Rudge wondered if— Impossible. The pair of ruffians who attacked him had been dead for hours before this man and his horses were shot. And they had come from the opposite direction. There might not be many people in this country, he reflected, but there was no shortage of bad ones.

The old man's face was suddenly as gray as his hair. Rudge guessed he shouldn't have given him a full swallow of water. But it was not that. The old man had been surviving hatless in the sun—existing on pure nerve. Now that help had arrived his wiry old body was extracting its dues.

He unrolled a blanket and strung it between junipers to give the old man more shade. Maclendon's hands and face changed abruptly from gray to bright pink. Rudge wet a bandanna and wiped him. He opened the shivering old man's shirt and inspected the wound. There had not been all that much bleeding. "You've an excellent chance of living," he said, "if we can get that bullet out and get you cooled off a bit. But I fancy you know you'll not ride thirty miles even if they are downhill."

"Guess not," Maclendon said fuzzily.

"Do you know who did it?"

"I know," the old man said grimly.

When it became obvious that he was not going to volunteer any more information, Rudge squatted on his heels beneath the scant shade and considered the gray-haired man.

"There are times when I suspect that I labor beneath a curse," he mused. "Shall I stay here and watch you die or shall I go down for help?"

"I ain't plannin' on dying just yet," the old man snapped. "When you get down there, tell 'em it's Maclendon."

Rudge nodded. "But what of your friends? Is it not possible that they might return?"

"Don't think so. Sons of bitches figured I was dead."

Rudge left a water bag and a box of crackers within the old man's reach. After a moment of internal debate he left the extra bottle of Green River. "Go easy on it," he said. "That's killed more men than ever lead put under."

"Ye wouldna' hae any real whusky, would ye?" Maclendon's almost-American suddenly backslid into broad Scots.

Rudge smiled and shook his head. "I'm afraid I've been too long from home for anything like that."

"Do ye hae a name?"

"Joseph Bentley Rudge. Now is there anything else I can do before I go?"

There was not. Maclendon's rifle was loaded. He was as comfortable as Rudge could make him. His wound no longer bled. "I'll move as fast as I can," Rudge promised. His horses had some mileage on them already. He considered hobbling the packhorse, then realized how easily a hobbled horse could die in this country if something went awry. He decided to lead the extra mustang and change mounts from time to time.

"Don't forget to say it's Maclendon," the old man called as Rudge was turning back once more toward Soda Springs.

By the time he had loped and trotted the indestructible mustangs back down into the basin the single street of Soda Springs was as dark as can be any town with neither street lights nor moon. He convinced himself that there was no one in the sheriff's office. Finally Rudge turned back to the only light in town—in the Golden Eagle where all his troubles had started. He tied up.

A half dozen men in broad-brimmed hats were at the bar. Four men sat at the table where Rudge had won a thousand dollars and done other things. A girl whose skirt rose nearly to her knees was first to recognize him. Silence spread in a ripple through the saloon. "The Limey in the funny hat," somebody muttered.

"Where might I find the sheriff?" Rudge asked.

The tension eased slightly. Abruptly Rudge realized that the Golden Eagle's patrons were not really trying to get behind him. They merely wanted to see what was strapped over his packhorse this time. "You go three doors down and cut in back through— Oh hell!" The bartender gave up.

"I'll go," the short-skirted girl said, and disappeared.

Rudge permitted himself the luxury of one short beer while he waited. Within minutes Sheriff Jason appeared, bleary-eyed and with sleep-tousled hair. One of his shirttails hung out. "I warned you once—" he began.

"I bear tidings from Maclendon."

For a moment it promised to turn into a waiting match, then the sheriff understood that Rudge was not in the habit of tripping over a wagging lip. "Go ahead," he growled.

"If you get a doctor and a wagon of some sort up there before he has to spend another day in the sun, perhaps you can save him. While you're at it you might find me a fresh horse. I'm afraid these are about used up."

The sheriff studied Rudge for a silent moment. Finally his face softened. "No need for you to go out again," he said. "You must've ridden close to a hundred miles."

"True," Rudge said. "But I'm somewhat delicate about the towns in which I sleep. And in any event, my kit is with Maclendon—whoever he may be."

No one volunteered any explanation.

The sheriff delegated several men to rouse the doctor and the livery stable hostler. Rudge finished his single beer and wondered if he was losing his ability to hold his liquor. But it was not one beer that had him suddenly seeing everything through two lengths of pipe. He wondered how many miles he had actually ridden since last he slept. He took several deep breaths and tensed muscles, doing his best not to show his fatigue before the inhabitants of the Golden Eagle.

Finally the expedition was ready and there was a fresh mount for Rudge—only a hand taller than the mustangs tied behind a buckboard that was fitted out with bows and canvas until it resembled a shallow-draft prairie schooner. Starting to ache, Rudge forced himself into the saddle and rode with the sheriff. The doctor, who was a silent man, drove the buckboard.

After he had nearly fallen off his mount a couple of times, Rudge tied the mustang along with his other two behind the buckboard and crawled inside. Despite the unsprung wagon's erratic progress from rock to rock, he slept until dawn awakened him.

He sat up blearily and tried to guess where they were. It was another hour before they found Rudge's camp and Maclendon. The gray-haired man was dead.

Rudge sighed. He found it difficult to be all that torn up over another dead stranger; yet he was puzzled, annoyed with himself for having given in to a charitable impulse that had done nothing for the old man, but had served to delay Rudge another day. Perhaps he should have stayed here and helped the old man through a difficult passage. But Maclendon hadn't seemed that bad off when Rudge had left. He began putting his kit back together while the doctor knelt over the rigid body.

"Why didn't you tell us he was shot?" the sheriff demanded.

Rudge studied the graying, walrus-mustached man in astonishment. "Would it have made any difference?" he asked. "It never occurred to my limited experience that anyone ever died of anything else in these parts."

Sheriff Jason turned the color of a freshly fired brick but he did not reply.

"It was the second shot did him in." The doctor had finally broken his nightlong silence.

Rudge turned. "Now that's rather odd."

"You're a doctor?" the medical man bridled.

"Not at all. But when I left, there was only one hole in him—rather high in the shoulder. Had there not been a reasonable hope for his recovery I'd not have made still another trip to a town of no special appeal to me."

"All right!" the sheriff snapped. "You've made your point!"

"Is his rifle still loaded?"

Jason checked the weapon. It was a .50-caliber Springfield and there was still an unfired round in the chamber.

"It's a single-shot weapon, isn't it?"

The sheriff gave Rudge an odd look and finally nodded.

Rudge went back to getting his kit together while the doctor and sheriff got Maclendon into the buckboard, onto the straw tick where Rudge had managed several hours of dreamless sleep.

Suddenly he became aware of doctor and sheriff studying him.

"You know who Maclendon was?"

"Mr. Jason," Rudge said tiredly, "I'm still unsure who you are. No one in this region volunteers information and if I have learned a single thing in my travels, it's that St. Paul's attitude was correct."

"Quit talkin' in circles!"

"When in Rome," the doctor exegesised.

"You know who shot him?"

"I asked."

"Did he know?"

"He assured me that he did."

"Well?"

"Well what?"

"Well who the hell was it?"

"Mr. Maclendon did not see fit to impart that information to me." Suddenly Rudge remembered something. He turned to examine the area around the swelling horse. "Fancy that," he muttered.

"Fancy what?"

"I left Mr. Maclendon an unopened bottle of Green River."

There was a brief silence. "Indians?" the doctor wondered.

"Mr. Maclendon was most emphatic that it was not."

"I mean the second time. Wound that killed him is several hours newer than the one in his shoulder."

"Knowing this," he demanded, "why am I the object of all your unwarranted suspicions?"

The sheriff produced a paper, which he carefully folded until it was only partly visible. He held it toward Rudge who read, "10,000 hd, get, chattels & real prop'ty."

"Can you read that?" the sheriff demanded.

"It's in English."

"What about the handwriting?"

It was an old man's hand, crabbed and shaky, but it showed its copperplate origins. "What do you wish to know?"

"Did the old man write it?"

Rudge stared at the sheriff. "Am I to divine a stranger's hand from the shape of a bullet hole?" he demanded. "What do you expect me to know about it?"

"Looks just like that note you sent me."

"Sent you?" Then Rudge remembered his good deed for the day. "That stripling who was attaching himself to me? What has he to do with this?"

"Nothing. But it's the same handwriting."

Rudge shrugged. "Mr. Maclendon was a Scotsman. No doubt he learned his reading and writing from the same sort of teachers as I."

"Still looks the same."

"Nonsense!" Rudge snapped. "We prefer the admittedly slower copperplate script. You colonials with your irrational drive for speed have been seduced by the loops and curlicues of a cursive hand. Spencerian may be faster to write but copperplate does the reader the courtesy of being readable. And of what does Mr. Maclendon's declaration accuse me? Did I kill him?"

"Nope," the sheriff said. "This paper don't accuse you of nothing. Just seems funny old Maclendon would go leavin' everything he owned to a stranger—'specially when he had family of his own."

"It's a strange country and you've filled it with even stranger people." Rudge turned back to his packing. Then abruptly he knew whom Maclendon had made his heir.

IV

It was shocking. Maclendon had not seemed crazy. Why would he cut off his family without even the proverbial shilling? Rudge faced the doctor and sheriff. "If I read you aright, Mr. Maclendon made over his holdings to me. Perhaps it's time now for you to read me. No matter how extensive, if this old man's property lies within fifty miles of Soda Springs, I'll decline and with no thanks. Rest assured that not even a change of sheriff could alter my intention to settle in some region where one does not drink water with a fork."

"You just coppered your bet by ten miles," the sheriff said dryly. "Maclendon's ranch is up thataway." He pointed in the direction Rudge had been heading. "But I'm sheriff up there too. Now let's get back down to town."

"Sorry."

"What do you mean, sorry?"

"The authorities told me my presence was unwelcome."

"God damn it! You want me to go out in the garden and eat worms?"

The doctor glanced from Rudge to the sheriff and kept his amusement to himself.

"Am I charged with some crime?" Rudge demanded.

"No."

"Then probate your own wills." Rudge went back to his packing. But as he turned away he was suddenly remembering the single line of spidery copperplate the sheriff had shown him. Then the sheriff's dry voice was echoing Rudge's thought. "What kind of man would walk away from ten thousand head?"

There was a moment of silence while Rudge put the finishing touches to his pack. He poured water into a gold pan and offered it to the mustangs who, being of Arab stock, treated water with proper respect and drank from the shallow pans without spilling. The sheriff studied the gold pan. "Somehow I'd never have taken you for a miner."

Rudge was tempted to remark that he would never have taken the other man for a sheriff.

"Be a hell of a mess for the family to straighten out," the sheriff said.

"I'll give you a quitclaim."

"'Tain't that," the sheriff said mournfully. "Anybody gets mixed up with Maclendon affairs is gonna need more than fancy words."

"I'm not for hire."

"Nope. I guess you ain't. You know, that kid you sent back to my office—he's one of Maclendon's family."

Rudge turned tiredly to face the sheriff. "What exactly is it you want of me?"

"Curious," Jason said. "Want to get to know you. Want to find out why Maclendon picked you over family—if he did. Folks called old Maclendon a lot of mean things while he was alive. But there was one thing nobody ever called him."

Rudge waited.

"Nobody ever called old Maclendon stupid," the sheriff elaborated. "Now will you *please* come back down to Soda Springs and help straighten this out?"

"Since you put it that way," Rudge said. He swung up onto his horse and waited for the buckboard to move out.

"Less dust up front," the sheriff said.

And less people behind me back here. But Rudge didn't say it. He just smiled and nodded, and let the buckboard stay in front.

By the time they were once more in Soda Springs it was

the doctor and the sheriff who were nodding and swaying. Rudge, after a night's bouncing in the buckboard, had recovered and watched the single street with his usual attention. They pulled up in front of Fine Furniture and Funerals. "Since you've induced me to return," Rudge said, "perhaps you could recommend lodgings?"

The sheriff pursed his lips as if this thought had never occurred to him. The doctor roused himself from a well of taciturnity and said, "Miz Bowman's."

Jason nodded. "'Bout the cleanest place in town," he said. Rudge rode down the street to the building they pointed out.

Mrs. Bowman was a broad-faced woman with a cheerful, no-nonsense air. Without asking, she directed a twelve-year-old boy with the same broad face to remove Rudge's impedimenta from the mustang and lead both horses to the livery stable. While Rudge stood on the front stoop, swaying slightly as he struggled to get used to being on his feet again, Mrs. Bowman directed a broad-faced girl to get water heating in the back yard.

Rudge roused himself. "You *heat* it?"

"Sody Springs water comes up cold as kraut," Mrs. Bowman said, and led him upstairs to a room. Rudge removed his dusty boots and stretched his lengthy body on a reasonably comfortable bed while the water heated. Immediately somebody was knocking on the door. He jerked awake and followed the broad-faced girl down the hall to another room, which was puzzling. Rudge had expected the bath to be brought to him, but instead, this room had a tin-lined tub permanently rigged to a drain that emptied onto a backyard garden.

He used nearly a cake of soap in the losing struggle with Soda Springs water while one of Mrs. Bowman's girls brushed his clothes and hung them to air. Finally Rudge gave up. He wiped alkali scum from his lanky body and wrapped himself in a California blanket for the journey down the hall. Halfway to his room he was interrupted by an opening door.

The head that emerged, unless Rudge was missing something, was attached to a remarkably well-constructed woman. She saw him clad only in a blanket and immediately retreated behind a closed door. Rudge went into his room and put on smallclothes. He stretched out on the bed and lit a cheroot.

He wondered idly if the common libels about red-haired women were true. But he wondered much more if he would not have lived a longer and happier life by keeping to the road. Rudge was as ready to believe in good luck as any man, and considering his genius for picking the losing side of any conflict, it was about time for his luck to change. But to inherit a ranch and ten thousand head from a total stranger who was not at odds with his family—Rudge had lost his belief in the tooth fairy early in 1864.

When he awoke to the sound of a dinner bell, his clothes had been returned to his room, somewhat improved with brushing and airing. He dressed and combed himself in a beginning-to-peel mirror. When he descended to the dining room the other guests were already passing platters.

There were perfunctory introductions to forgettable boarders and Rudge tucked into a remarkably good meal, considering the distance from Soda Springs to the nearest green vegetable. The red-haired young lady he had met in the hallway was not present. He devoted himself to the stew, which, thanks to some culinary magic, contained large chunks of beef less chewy than the local water. And despite the alkalinity of its basis, Mrs. Bowman had even managed to produce drinkable coffee.

From the deference shown him at table Rudge knew his reputation had preceded him. He wondered if the Bowman establishment often catered to guests with questionable credentials.

There being no apparent church in Soda Springs, funeral services were graveside in the cool of early next morning. Attendance, to Rudge, was disconcerting. The doctor and the sheriff nodded to him. There were four wooden chairs beside the hole. Two were empty.

Rudge studied the backs of a young man and woman in the other two and after a moment realized they were the young redhead, who had surprised him in the hallway, and the boy he had sent back to the sheriff as his good deed for the day. A waxy-skinned young preacher coughed and stumbled over the eulogy. The preacher was a lunger and seemed mildly surprised—as if he had expected the tough old man to bury *him*.

Tell them it's Maclendon. Had the old man an exaggerated opinion of his own importance—or were the townspeople . . . Rudge remembered his first morning ride into Soda Springs. They had all gotten up early to get their chores done before the heat.

Tell them it's Maclendon. The old man hadn't said he was popular or beloved—only that his name would be known. The preacher coughed and stumbled on and finally it was over. The boy and the doctor helped the young redhead to her feet. She tossed something into the hole and turned away. Abruptly Rudge saw that she was not overcome with grief. Man and boy were helping because she was some kind of a cripple. She held her entire body rigid from the waist up. Rudge sighed and turned away. Too bad it had to be such a pretty woman.

"Mr. Rudge?"

He turned back. It was the young woman. The boy beside her was struggling to pretend that he did not know Rudge.

"It was you who found my father?"

"I fancy so, miss, assuming your father was Mr. Maclendon."

"There will be a reading of the will this afternoon," she

said in a toneless voice. Before he could reply the boy and the doctor whisked her away.

Rudge stood a moment longer watching a dyspeptic-appearing man nearly as tall and lean as himself shoveling dry, gravelly dirt into the hole. Finally he turned and lit a cheroot as he strolled toward the livery stable.

"Yessir! Leavin' already?" the hostler asked.

"No such luck," Rudge said as he put out his cheroot. "Just dropped by to look in on my horses." The mustangs seemed rested and well fed, none the worse for their marathon runs in and out of Soda Springs. He studied the hostler who had apparently decided Rudge was not going to shoot him on the spot. "The sheriff assures me these horses are now mine," he said. "Could you tell me anything of their previous owners?"

The hostler shrugged and spat tobacco. "The baldface belonged to one of them you brung in."

"I suspected as much." Rudge wondered if the hostler was attempting a witticism, or if he was just simple.

The hostler shrugged and spat again. "Bunch of trash hangs out at the Golden Eagle. Way I heerd it you won a couple of pots there. I s'pose one of them wanted it back."

Obviously, Rudge was going to learn nothing new here. "Do you know anything of the young man on the other horse?"

"Some no-count drifter. Seems like this country's really gone to hell since't the war. Ain't nobody puts a strop to their young'uns any more."

"Who was Maclendon?"

The hostler gave him an odd look. "Didn't you help bring him in?"

"I did. But I still don't know who he was."

"Rancher. Had some land up west of here. Hear he's been havin' a spell of trouble lately. Guess he won't have no more."

To this Rudge could offer no dissenting opinion. He

thanked the hostler and lit another cheroot as he wondered how he was going to kill the rest of the morning. The Golden Eagle was the only game in town, and even if somebody in that den of iniquity didn't try to backshoot him, he doubted if it would be possible to get up a game now that the locals knew he was not an easy mark.

As he stepped from the livery stable he saw a striped pole across the street. From the sudden silence as he stepped in, Rudge knew his reputation had also preceded him here. Two customers waiting were both eager to surrender their turn to him.

"I'll wait," Rudge said. But when the others began remembering urgent appointments he took pity on the barber and sat in the chair.

"You know, I don't devour small children alive," he said through lather.

"Nothin' against you personal, Mister Limejuice," one client said. "I just don't want to get in the way." He slipped out the door.

Rudge sighed and composed his hands beneath the towel as the chair tilted back. "How do you get up a lather with this water?" he asked.

The barber gave a nervous laugh. "I can see by the scum in your hair," he said, "that nobody told you about that boxful of sody-ash next to the tin tub. You stir in a handful and then skim it off before you try to use any soap. Same thing with clothes unless you want to use your pantslegs for stilts."

To Rudge it seemed odd that adding more alkali would make the waters of Soda Springs endurable. But he had heard of similar alchemies in the boilers of locomotives.

The barber was just getting ready for the first stroke with the razor when his hesitation warned Rudge. But it was a false alarm. A man with his face shadowed beneath a droop-brim hat peered in the door and changed his mind. Rudge and the barber relaxed.

"Is that someone I ought to know about?" Rudge asked when the barber was brushing his neck.

"I got to live in this town."

"May settle here myself," Rudge teased.

"Good luck," the barber said. "Good luck to you and the sheriff."

Rudge handed him two bits and strolled back to Mrs. Bowman's, devoting his usual meticulous attention to any sign of unexpected movement along the street. But nothing happened. He arrived just in time for the dinner bell. Once more the young redhead was not at the table.

Rudge dedicated himself to corned beef and sauerkraut, followed by dried apple pie. He was burning another cheroot on the front stoop when his good deed appeared. Struggling for a noncommittal face, the boy said, "They're gonna read the will."

"Will they now?" Rudge got to his feet and followed the boy who walked stiff-legged past the sheriff's office toward a false-front attorney-at-law office.

"Be of good cheer," Rudge said to the boy's back. "I didn't travel very far without you now, did I?" But the boy was still not disposed to forgive Rudge's dastardly betrayal of him to the forces of reaction. They went into the office and took chairs. The young redheaded woman was already there, sitting stiff as Lydia E. Pinkham on a canebottom chair. Sheriff Jason arrived a moment later.

The lawyer was young and waxy-skinned as the preacher, with bright red spots on each cheek. Rudge realized with a start that half the population of Soda Springs must be lungers. All the more reason to move on away from bad water, bungling law, and stiff-sitting women. He spun as the door opened but it was only the doctor.

"Guess we're ready," the lawyer began in a diffident voice. When nobody objected he ran rapidly through a spate of formalities about sound mind and *articulo mortis*. Rudge wondered how a dying Scotsman could have found time for all this wordage.

He listened to something about ten thousand head, get, chattels, and real property, waiting for the waxy-skinned lawyer to deal the joker. When it came nobody was surprised. "To be held in joint tenancy by my son, Malcolm Maclendon, and my daughter, Mrs. Agnes Lowery, said estate to be administered and one-third ownership vested in Joseph Bentley Rudge pending Malcolm's majority and Agnes' disentanglement from matrimonial encumberances."

So the stiff-bodied young lady with the abundant red hair and nice face was married. Why wasn't Mr. Lowery here? Why was Rudge?

He sighed, realizing that if he'd had a father-in-law who wasted his dying moments in insult, Rudge too might have made himself scarce from any reading of a will. Not that it made any difference. He reached for his black *sevillano* hat. "I'll give you a quitclaim, Mrs. Lowery," he assured the redheaded young woman.

Mrs. Lowery glanced up at him in surprise.

"Even if I were to demand a share," Rudge explained, "any will which encourages murder, or any less-definitive dissolution of matrimonial bonds, is patently illegal. Please convey my heartfelt sympathy to Mr. Lowery."

The waxy-skinned young man was startled. "You've read law, Mr. Rudge?"

"At Cambridge."

"But you don't sound like a Yankee. I thought you were English."

"By an odd coincidence, there's also a Cambridge in England."

From the young man's mystification it was obvious that his historical knowledge began somewhere post-Massachusetts. Rudge took pity on him. He put his *sevillano* on, bowed to the red-haired Mrs. Lowery, turned back to the lawyer, and said, "Just draw up the papers. I'll sign anything, providing it's spelled properly."

"No." Mrs. Lowery's voice was firm.

Rudge stopped. "You wish to give away one third of your patrimony?"

"My husband is dead, Mr. Rudge. One impediment gone. But my brother has yet to attain his majority. I shall welcome your aid in administering the estate."

V

For once Rudge was at a loss for words. "You know nothing of me," he protested. "Don't you realize this half-baked document allows me to steal you blind? I can swallow the entire estate and charge it off to administration fees."

For some obscure reason the sheriff was now amused. He put on his hat and opened the door. "Good luck," he said, and disappeared.

Rudge stared at the young lawyer who stared back. He studied the red-haired woman. Her brother had finally forgotten his huff and waited. "You're distraught," Rudge finally managed. "I'll not hold you to this." To the lawyer he said, "Draw up those papers. We can discuss this later when everyone has calmed down."

"Everyone is calm, Mr. Rudge," the redhead said.

"I'm not." Rudge bowed, put his hat on, and made his escape.

It was the hottest part of the afternoon and the single street was deserted. He skulked from shadow to shade along the wooden walkway, trying to decipher what was happening. As a youth Rudge had read improbable novels in which ragged boys rescued the daughters of railroad magnates from runaway horses and were rewarded in this fashion. But even as a boy Rudge had known that the real world does not work this way—that no matter how elegant the snack in the saloon, there ain't no free lunch.

Somebody had killed Maclendon. Mrs. Lowery expected more trouble. Rudge supposed that he appeared perhaps a shade less larcenous than any local would-be champion. He had bested two or three local reputations. Ergo, he was an expert. He gave a thin-lipped smile as he recalled some philosopher's definition of that word: an expert is some son of a bitch from out of town.

"Mr. Rudge!"

He turned. It was the Maclendon boy. Now what was his name? "Yes? Malcolm, isn't it?"

"Please do it."

Rudge sighed. "Do you know what you're asking?" When the boy did not reply, he continued, "If you're so eager for me to take charge, why were you ready to abandon your sister a day or two ago?"

There was an instant's hesitation, then the boy said, "Papa was alive then."

Rudge hadn't considered that. "It would make a difference," he conceded. But neither of old Maclendon's offspring seemed particularly down in the mouth about the old man's passing. Rudge remembered when he had learned of his own father's death. Even now he did not like to think about it.

"Will you?"

Rudge sighed and remembered an older companion in arms *down there* who had given him advice for a lifetime: "They's only two things I'm afeard of—a decent woman and being left afoot." Since arriving at Soda Springs, Rudge had lost his horse. He shuddered.

Back at Mrs. Bowman's he finally escaped from the boy by explaining that civilized people always sleep through this part of the afternoon. He locked his door and stretched out on the bed as he tried to think.

Rudge was reaching an age when he could no longer trust in boyish charm—when he was beginning to rely perhaps too much on a pair of altered Colts. He had to settle down somewhere. What was it like at the other, snow-pointing end of the tilted plain that bottomed out at Soda Springs?

He reminded himself that he was invited only to manage

an estate. It was not as if the rigid Mrs. Lowery would make any demands on his person. Even if she were to turn kittenish, surely he was still agile enough to escape the clutches of a good woman.

Next morning, abundant red hair piled high in braided coils, Mrs. Lowery appeared for breakfast. Rudge noted that at this hour she seemed a trifle more flexible. She greeted him and the other boarders with the same restraint. Rudge saw the boy's eagerness and knew his sister must have tightened the young man's checkrein several notches, for after breakfast, there was no pursuit when he strolled down to the livery stable to look to his mustangs.

This morning the hostler was sewing harness. There were two buckboards and a freighting wagon next to the corral and a young man struggled with a wagon jack. Rudge wondered if ever Soda Springs water could wash the black axle-grease stains from the young man's shirt. "Someone going traveling?" he asked.

The hostler looked up from the leather tubing he was stitching around a chain trace. "You don't know 'em?" When Rudge assured him that he did not, the hostler grinned. "Them's your wagons."

Yesterday the hostler had been afraid of Rudge. Today he seemed amused. Rudge managed not to show his annoyance. He considered walking from shadow to shade and decided that, even if there were not other attendant risks in visiting the Golden Eagle, a cool beer was not really worth the trip. He returned to Mrs. Bowman's.

This time Mrs. Lowery sat on the front stoop, wedged tightly with cushions into a ladder-back chair. She was studying an open ledger. She saw him and nodded from the neck up.

Rudge snagged the next rocker and sat, fanning himself with his stiff-brimmed *sevillano*. "You ordered those wagons at the livery stable?"

"Yes, Mr. Rudge." She handed him the ledger.

He was about to say that he had still not accepted, when he remembered he was getting too old for reluctant-virgin roles. He ran through the estate accounts. "What are these DB entries in the 'wages' column?" he finally asked. "Any debit should be itemized."

"They are," Mrs. Lowery said. "DB is not an abbreviation for debit."

"Oh?"

"Death benefit," she explained.

Should have guessed. Rudge had known he was not being offered one third of an estate because of his scintillating personality. He went through the columns of figures again, making a mental note to learn what some of these other odd abbreviations meant. Dip, cut, P. & L. were fairly obvious. Now what on earth was *trsq?*

He shrugged. Those things could be gone into later. What mattered was the bottom line. He turned to Mrs. Lowery. "One is expected not to look a gift horse in the mouth," he said. "But the most cursory of glances demonstrates a total lack of teeth in this one."

"Exactly," the red-haired woman said. "Father was getting old. The Maclendon holdings are badly in need of some teeth. You seem at loose ends, Mr. Rudge, as are many of your kind who drift this way." Rudge gave her a sharp glance but Mrs. Lowery blandly continued, "If you can produce the necessary teeth, your rewards may prove substantial."

"Such honesty is refreshing," Rudge said. "Whom and how many?"

"I beg your pardon?"

"Whom and how many do I kill?"

He had been prepared for the usual flurry of delicacy and disclaimers. When the magnificent redhead did not blink, it was Rudge who was suddenly uncertain.

"That is my expected function, is it not?"

"Yes, Mr. Rudge."

"Why are you so certain I'll join your side?"

"Because there are sides. The whole country is rapidly choosing up."

It took Rudge an instant to understand her oblique reference to that odd, cricketlike game that farm boys sometimes played in this country. "But I could still pick the wrong side," he said, remembering that he had done so twice.

"I'm afraid you've already picked, Mr. Rudge."

"Because I tried to save a stranger's life?"

"Only partly. You see, before that you had already killed two of my father's enemies."

Now why hadn't Rudge thought of that? He wondered how many more unseen facets would come to light. "But everything I've learned so far," he said, "would impel a discreet man to seek greener pastures."

"Are you a discreet man, Mr. Rudge?" Irrelevantly, she added, "As a child I attended school in the East. At that time my father had holdings in Kansas."

A bit of a scare shot through Rudge. He studied her from the corner of his eye and told himself he was imagining things. Mrs. Lowery could not be past her early twenties. Ten years ago . . . "By the way"—he struggled to make it casual—"have you been widowed long?"

Mrs. Lowery considered the question for a moment, then began counting on her fingers.

"Three years?" he asked.

"No, Mr. Rudge. Three days."

Rudge struggled to cover his confusion. "I fancy many of the weak-lunged seek out Soda Springs's climate," he managed.

Mrs. Lowery gave a vague murmur and the silence lay heavy. He searched for something to say. "And how is the climate up at the Maclendon estate?" he finally managed.

"Deadly, Mr. Rudge. But the countryside is very pleasant if one can live to enjoy it."

"Will you return?"

"Would you spend the rest of your life here?"

"At the risk of offending the locals," he began. To his surprise this elicited the first hint of a smile that he had ever seen in any Maclendon.

An elderly boarder with brown stains at the corners of his beard emerged from the house and took possession of an empty Boston rocker. "Nice day," he said.

Rudge refrained from looking Mrs. Lowery in the eye as he soberly agreed. Beyond the Bowman front stoop heat rose in shimmering waves. He gladly surrendered the conversation to the old man whose memories of the war were at such variance to Rudge's that it was some time before Rudge realized the old man referred to an older and smaller war with Mexico.

There were obviously hidden currents in the Maclendon family. He wondered how anyone with such an abundance of coiled red hair could be such a cold fish. But he reminded himself that Mrs. Lowery carried herself much too stiffly for even the most prim of ladies. Pain might have altered her perceptions. The old man was gabbing away about the day he had marched with General Wool into a Monterrey a generation newer than the fought-over rubble of Rudge's memory. He supposed he ought to ask Mrs. Lowery how soon they would be leaving Soda Springs but the old man was not about to relinquish an audience. Rudge made his escape under the pretext of smoking a cheroot at a nonpolluting distance from all that red hair.

Abruptly he sensed a sudden air of expectancy along the town's single street. After the first scent of tension Rudge sensed that for once he was apparently not the focal point of this latest break in the municipal monotony.

A lean, sun-bronzed rider cantered into town on a drooping horse, heading straight for the livery stable. The bartender of the Golden Eagle stood before his saloon, his white apron conspicuous among the other gawkers. The proprietor of the Mercantile was looking out his door. Then Rudge heard the distant jingle and creak of harness. Four freight wagons were creeping into town.

"No trouble this time?" the hostler shouted.

The lead teamster shook his head as he coiled his whip. He was heading for the Golden Eagle when his eyes met Rudge's and held for an instant. There was the tiniest hint of hesitation, then the teamster was once more striding toward the relative coolness of the saloon.

Rudge riffled through his memory and could find no recollection. He sighed. Nobody could remember everyone whose path crossed his. Maybe the other man had decided it was not the same man after all. Rudge moved farther back into the shade and watched as locals helped the freighters to discharge cargo.

Many of the sacks and barrels were being passed directly from one wagon to another. As smaller loads were stowed in the pair of canvas-hooped buckboards he finally understood what Mrs. Lowery had been waiting here in town for. Which reminded him . . .

He turned back toward the boardinghouse and met the redhead moving slowly and stiffly beneath a parasol. She was heading toward the livery stable, which was apparently also the local harness and saddlery combined with freight terminal. "Right away?" he asked.

"Yes, Mr. Rudge."

He hunted for some diplomatic way to put it, couldn't find any, and decided not to ask if Mrs. Lowery's infirmity would permit her to travel any distance in a buckboard. "Is there anything I can do at the moment?" he asked.

"You might settle up with Mrs. Bowman so we can get a decent distance out of town before nightfall."

Rudge nodded and tipped his hat. He was turning to walk the hundred yards back to the boardinghouse when he saw the teamster who had stared at him. The burly man was heading for the sheriff's office.

VI

Rudge tried to put it from his mind. Nobody could remember everything. The burly teamster was now peering
through the window into an obviously empty sheriff's office.
Now where was the sheriff? Was he the only man in town
who had not turned out to watch the arrival of the
freighters?

Mrs. Bowman accepted three dollars and wished him
Godspeed. Rudge cleaned and oiled his altered Colts,
packed his kit, and was dragging it onto the front stoop just
as his good deed—Malcolm—pulled up in front with one of
the buckboards. "I'll load your stuff," the boy offered. "Got
to get ours too." Before Rudge could thank him, the boy
continued, "Aggie says for you to git on down to the livery
stable and move that wagon out."

When Rudge arrived the freighting wagon was hitched to
six mustangs. He considered the size of the horses and the
straight sixty miles of uphill trail with some foreboding. But
this couldn't be the first time. It behooved him to remember
that anyone who lived around here ought to know more
about the road than he did.

Rigid as a flagpole, Mrs. Lowery stood in the scant shade
of the livery stable amid half-loaded supplies. "The wagon
is slower than the buckboards," she said. "It might expedite
matters if you were to leave at once."

"It's ready?"

"Yes, Mr. Rudge. Please hurry."

Why was she in such an infernal hurry? He wished he
were as ready as the wagon. He tried to remember when last

he had driven six horses. He sorted out the reins, putting leads between thumb and forefinger, wheelers at the bottom of the deck. With luck he could get the team turned and heading out of town without disgracing himself. He shook the reins and clucked.

The horses began the turn sedately enough, but in spite of the midday heat something in their mustang nature—or perhaps in Rudge's stale hands—was enough to set them off. Halfway through the turn the horses began galloping.

He gritted his teeth and braced for a spill. The wagon careened up on two wheels for an instant, then straightened and began rattling up the single street. He supposed he ought to be swearing and sawing at the reins but the road lay straight for over a mile. It was also uphill. If the horses wanted to run away this was as good a place for it as any. He caught a glimpse of sheriff and teamster from the corner of his eye. Both men stared at the runaway.

The freight wagon was jouncing alarmingly. His hat flew off and landed somewhere amid the load piled beneath the canvas bows. His Colts were slamming up and down against his thighs and Rudge was in contact with the seat only half the time.

He had already passed the last house and was on the trail proper. The wagon hit a sandy stretch and sunk in past the fellies. The horses were lathered but still they galloped. He was about to give up and saw them to a halt when he noted that a near mile of uphill had finally dampened their enthusiasm. Another hundred yards and they were trotting. Six mustangs slowed to a walk and wanted to stop.

He cracked the whip and forced the heaving beasts to cool out for another half mile before he indulged them. "Hope you learned your lesson," he growled, knowing these flighty beasts could be counted on never to learn anything until it was too late.

When he was convinced the mustangs were too winded for any more monkeyshines he tied the reins to the brake

pole and scrambled back inside long enough to recover his
sevillano. Peering through the dark tunnel of canvas, he
studied the trail back toward Soda Springs. There was nobody following. No buckboards, no sheriff.

He squinted at the sun. An hour past noon, he guessed.
How many times had he covered this piece of trail? He
clucked and slapped reins until the mustangs began walking. Maybe he should have held them in. They seemed
exhausted now.

Once out and into an ambush.

Once back in with two bodies.

Back out again with a new supply of water.

Back in again to get help for Maclendon.

Out again with sheriff and doctor.

In again with Maclendon's body.

This was his seventh passage over this piece of trail.
"Couple more times and a man could learn to hate this
place," he growled. Two mustangs replied from the ends
that faced him.

He cracked his whip but the horses couldn't, or wouldn't,
move any faster. It was going to be a long journey, but at
least the rambunctiousness was worked out of them and
the lead team seemed to have enough sense to follow the
trail. He tilted his hat against the sun and struggled to find
some position that would not grind more flesh from lean
buttocks. The rocking wagon bench gradually turned into
an instrument of torture.

The next time the horses had to blow he hunted through
the freight for something soft. A sack of flour would put his
feet clear off the dashboard and would not be that much
softer than the plank. He sighed and resigned himself.

Behind him Soda Springs was still in view. Two tiny spots
of white were visible just beyond the edge of town. The
buckboards, he supposed. It would be hours before they
caught up. The mustangs were tossing their heads and
stamping.

"If you've got that much ginger you may as well be pulling," he muttered and cracked the whip. It was only after they had strained the heavy wagon into motion that he saw what was making the horses uneasy. He snapped his whip at it, wondering what a sidewinder was doing out this time of day. The snake wound off into the shade of another juniper. Rudge searched for some other way to lessen the grinding between the wagon bench and his too-lean buttocks. He wondered how the rigid Mrs. Lowery was making out.

He ran his hand over the scab where the bullet had creased his head. Not too far from here, he guessed. Which reminded him that whoever had killed Maclendon was still loose somewhere in this territory. He had looked for a brand on the buckboards and freight wagon back down in the livery stable. There was none. He should have asked Mrs. Lowery. It would be helpful to know what brand he was working for. Should also, he guessed, have asked the red-haired woman how many other brands there were up ahead. Did it ever cool off in this country?

A half hour passed and once more it was the horses who warned Rudge. Was he getting old or was it just the heat? But he had been in hot country down there and kept his wits about him. If he didn't tend to business and keep his eyes open here . . .

Four men rode in columns of twos, coming downtrail toward his laboring mustangs. As they came within rifle range the men spread out in flank formation. Rudge halted his team and tied the reins to the brake pole. "Back together!" he roared, and drew one Colt. He gripped the huge weapon in both fists and aimed at the man in the center.

Immediately the man he was aiming at raised his hands. "That's downright unfriendly," he called.

"At your inquest I shall explain to the citizens of this county that spreading out is prima facie evidence of hostility. Now call your men back together with their hands in plain sight and we shall analyze your possibly pacific intentions."

To Rudge's intense relief the bluff worked. The outriders bunched in on the man he was aiming at and they continued riding until they were so close he stood a fair chance of actually hitting one of them with the Colt.

"Who in hell are you?" the man he aimed at asked. He was a large man, with a beefy red face that reminded Rudge of the man he had faced in that poker game at the Golden Eagle. The others were practically touching him now, sitting their horses like clay pigeons in a row.

Rudge did not lower the pistol. "I am a stranger with peaceable intentions," he said, "whose right of innocent passage has been interfered with once too often on this stretch of road."

"'Fraid that ain't good enough, stranger," the beefy man said with a hint of a smile. "People that ride this trail can only head for one out of two places."

"One of them presumably being San Francisco?"

The beefy man stared a moment, then laughed. "Not any more," he said. "Railroad's a couple of hundred miles north of here. Besides, you ain't goin' to drive them mustangs clear across the mountains."

In the press of events Rudge had forgotten momentarily that he no longer sat his gray. He braced himself on the bench of the freight wagon and wondered if the mustangs would be tired enough not to fight the brake. Maybe he should have drawn the reins tighter.

The man at the right end of the flank was having trouble with a horse that sensed the tension and was prancing. As it half turned Rudge caught a glimpse of an odd $\bigcirc$o brand like a penny-farthing bicycle. "Please indulge a stranger," he asked. "What's the name of your brand and who owns it?"

"Now that's downright funny," the beefy man growled. Rudge supposed that looking into the muzzle of a Colt was finally eroding his good humor. Then he knew better when the other continued, "You're freightin' for Maclendon."

Rudge did not reply.

"Funniest part of it is you don't know the Oostenveld Double-O brand."

"Should I?"

"You might look at one of them horses you're drivin'. Where'd you get him?"

"A stranger killed my horse," Rudge explained. "He was so cut up about it that he gave me his."

The man on the prancing horse was edging away from the others. "Will you be first, or the fat one in the middle?" Rudge asked.

There was a sudden explosion of action as all four went for their guns. Rudge blew the end man out of the prancing horse's saddle. He got off another shot at the man who had been doing the talking but flinching horses spoiled his aim. He rolled off the high wagon box as lead shrieked through just-vacated space.

He landed heavier than he would have preferred, crunching into the sandy ground next to the front wheel. The mustangs were lunging and screaming now and in spite of a set brake the wagon was groaning ahead. Just in time he scrambled out of the path of a six-foot-high back wheel.

Three men were shooting blindly into and under the wagon. Rudge debated whether to clamber on it or— Instead, he jumped backward off the trail and was half-concealed behind a clump of juniper by the time the wagon had moved out of the way.

He shot one of the men who seemed to think he was still hiding under the wagon. He fired rapidly again and was sure that this time he had hit the beefy talker too, but suddenly the two survivors were galloping away, totally demoralized by fire from an unexpected direction.

Rudge was breathing raggedly, still half-breathless from his awkward landing off the high wagon seat. He reloaded his guns and picked up his hat. A hundred yards ahead the mustangs were kicking and struggling against the brake-set wagon. He began trotting after the wagon, wondering if there was any real hope of catching up before those half-broken beasts spilled the wagon and tore up the harness.

If they had been fresh beasts struggling against the dead weight of a brake-set wagon it would have been a different story. But these beasts had already run away once today. The wagon was still upright when he caught hold of the tailgate and swung aboard to scramble under the canvas up to the seat. He managed to untie the reins and release the brake. With the wagon free the mustangs stopped kicking and started running.

Rudge supposed he ought to stop them. There might be somebody still alive behind him. He balanced charity against practicality and knew that without another runaway it could have taken him an extra hour to travel this far. He wondered how the imperturbable Mrs. Lowery would react to two bodies in the trail. He sighed.

Scrambling about had knocked the scab off the wound on his head. He had torn some skin off an elbow and an elbow out of his shirt. Damn this gravelly country! The horses slowed and wanted to stop. He made a highly original suggestion and cracked the whip. "Insist on running away," he said and added, "You might as well wear yourselves out. But don't come up lame on me when we're not even halfway across this desert." When the horses did not reply, he continued, "Just keep trotting another uphill mile and maybe you'll learn."

Sweat was pouring from the panicked beasts. He kept them trotting for another minute, then let the mustangs drop down to a walk. Poor beasts. They would never learn. Couldn't. Could Rudge?

"How else could I have handled it?" he muttered.

"*A soft answer turneth away wrath*," his recording angel replied.

"Can it turn away bullets?"

"They that live by the sword shall die by the sword," his angel countered.

"But you can hardly fault me for trying to postpone it."

"You could at least turn back and make sure they're dead. What if Mrs. Lowery and the boy were to come upon one of them still alive enough to shoot?"

Rudge raised his eyebrows to heaven. "Perhaps you could help me turn six horses on a trail that's not even wide enough for this motherless wagon?" For once he sensed that he had scored a point against his recording angel.

The trail straightened and he stood on the seat to look back. The battlefield was out of sight—or maybe still visible, but he could not tell where it had happened even though the trail was visible practically back down to Soda Springs. He squinted and thought he saw the white canvas of the buckboards a few miles behind. Facing ahead once more, he saw the sun would be down in another hour. He began peeling his eye for someplace to make camp.

VII

The sun's disc was half-hidden behind the snowcapped mountains before he found a place that seemed hard enough for the wagon not to sink in. He pulled off the trail and scanned the tailgate for hobbles. They were not there. On his knees he searched to see if they were wrapped round the hounds. The hobbles turned up in the box under the seat. He unharnessed the mustangs. After two runaways and thirty miles uphill into the sun they seemed finally to have lost their penchant for equine mischief. He hunted feed and guessed it must be in the buckboards. From the wagon box he could see them a couple of miles behind. He found an ax and used the last of the daylight to shatter brittle pieces of dead paloverde and mezquite.

The buckboards caught up. Mrs. Lowery sat rigid on the leading wagon, every strand of red hair still in place. Rudge stared in mild amazement until he saw how totally colorless was her face. He stepped forward to help her down. She leaned toward him. Her lean body kept right on leaning. Rudge was so startled that she nearly knocked him down. At the last possible minute he realized what was happening and managed to break her fall.

The boy hurried up from the trailing buckboard. Between them they got a blanket on the ground and Rudge's tailcoat beneath her red hair. Rudge was plowing through his kit in the buckboard looking for whiskey, when she finally managed a croaking, "Can't imagine what's come over me."

"It's called sunstroke," Rudge said. "Otherwise known as

exhaustion. Do you claim an immunity to the slings and arrows of outrageous fortune?"

"No, Mr. Rudge. Neither slings, arrows, nor bullets."

Rudge guessed that Agnes Lowery's life in this country might in ways have been as adventuresome as his own. Her brother was also near the end of his tether after a day on a buckboard seat. Rudge left him to unharness and hobble the buckboard teams while he rummaged through supplies, got a fire going, and performed the minimum requirements on beef and corn pone.

When the fire was banked and supper simmering, he turned to study the wan and silent Mrs. Lowery. After a moment's hesitation he went to the buckboard and rummaged in his kit again until he found the Green River. He poured a generous slug into a tin cup, considered the proprieties and probabilities, and added an equal quantity of the liquid that passed for water in Soda Springs. He returned to where she lay on the blanket and knelt to help her sit up. "What is it?" she asked.

"Medicine. It has a rather bad taste, so you'd best gulp it quick."

Mrs. Lowery followed instructions, choked a moment, and some color returned to her face. "Really, Mr. Rudge," she gasped, "there was no need to spoil it with that awful water."

Rudge bowed. "I stand corrected," he said, and looked to the corn pone. By the time he had dished up three plates Mrs. Lowery was somewhat recovered. "How odd," she said.

"Odd?"

"That you should prefer corn pone to the usual wheaten bread of your countrymen."

"When in Rome," Rudge shrugged. "In any event, I spent some time South."

"The Confederacy?" There was a warning note of disapproval.

"Farther south," Rudge said. "Amid the disintegrating remnants of His Catholic Majesty's *imperio*."

"That will be helpful."

"In what way?"

"*¿Habla español?*"

"Oh yes. Unavoidably."

"Many of our hands do not speak English."

"I see." Abruptly Rudge realized he had been so exhausted he had actually forgotten. "Er—" He wondered how to phrase it. "Did you perchance encounter anything unusual on the trail today?"

"Unusual, Mr. Rudge?"

He glanced at the boy. Malcolm Maclendon was almost asleep. "There was no novelty along the trail?" he insisted.

"I can think of nothing, Mr. Rudge. Perhaps I should have been more attentive."

So somebody had doubled back and picked up the men he had shot this afternoon. One was dead for sure. He wondered about the other. "Do you know a brand like a penny-farthing bicycle?"

"A what?"

"A large circle and a small one."

"You must mean the Oostenveld."

"Your enemies?"

"You might say that."

"I sincerely hope so," Rudge said. "Four of them jumped me."

"Oh? Did they—mistreat you?"

"Two of them got away."

"I see," Mrs. Lowery said reflectively.

The moon, if he was counting correctly, would not be up before early morning. Rudge considered the boy and the woman. He had enjoyed two good nights' sleep at Mrs. Bowman's, so he readied himself for the first watch.

"Please call me before my brother," Mrs. Lowery murmured, then surrendered to the whiskey.

Rudge sat with his back to the dying fire, listening to the rustle and slither as the desert's inhabitants came awake. It turned cool and he draped a blanket over his shoulders. He wondered if Mrs. Lowery was a cold fish or if she had just seen too much too soon in this unpredictable country. He reminded himself that she had only been widowed three—or was it four days now? Couldn't have been the most ideal of marriages, he supposed. But Mrs. Lowery was Scottish. A heart could break just as easily even when not worn on the sleeve. Perhaps a Scottish heart was even more fragile. Otherwise, why go to such trouble to conceal it?

He had always been at a loss to understand them. An unfeeling, oatmeal-devouring rabble. Yet those Rudge had known were openhearted. They were often desperately poor, but Scots hospitality was a long call from the groveling suspicion of the peasantry he had seen in England.

Somewhere behind him a coyote began tuning up. Within minutes they were in full voice. Odd-flying birds flitted through the dark sky and abruptly he saw they were bats. He heard the tiny whistling shriek that meant some rabbit's inoffensive life had been sacrificed to maintain the desert's power structure. And somewhere near the back door of his mind he could hear the gentle knock of his recording angel. "Please," he begged, "not tonight."

An hour passed, then Mrs. Lowery said, "You may as well try to rest, Mr. Rudge."

"And you?"

"I'm afraid I've slept as long as I will tonight."

He remembered how near collapse she had been earlier. "Are you in pain?" he asked.

"I beg your pardon?"

"Do you hurt?"

"No more than usual." There was a pause. "You may have noted my rigid gait," she said musingly. "Please be assured the injury is not of long standing. Within a fortnight I should return to normal."

"I see." Rudge was suddenly afraid the darkness might make him the recipient of confidences he did not truly wish to receive. "Do you have a firearm?" he asked.

"A rifle." She paused. "Which often damages me as much as the object at which I shoot."

"They were not made for women of slight constitution," he agreed. The capable redhead was sitting with her blanket over her shoulders, so he lay down in his own to await the renewable blessing of sleep. Immediately somebody was shaking him.

"Mr. Rudge," she murmured, "I have reason to believe someone is approaching."

"Downtrail?" he whispered, then he heard the creak of leather and the jingle of a bridle. It sounded like a single rider. Hastily he pulled on his boots and looked to his Colts. Mrs. Lowery crept to where her brother slept and put a hand over his mouth while she urged him into awareness.

The moon had still not risen, but the fire had been out for hours and Rudge's sleep-restored eyes no longer saw only tiny dazzling explosions of sunlight. He studied the angle of the Big Dipper and guessed it still lacked an hour or two of dawning. The horse came slowly nearer.

Rudge squinted at the canvas-covered buckboards and the immense freight wagon, wondering how far that billow of whiteness would be visible by starlight. He felt in his pocket for extra ammunition, wondered if just once in this country the interruption would turn out to be a peaceable traveler who was not intent on forcing Rudge to do what he had learned to do too well. Still the single horse loped closer. Then abruptly he heard the change of gait as someone pulled the horse to a halt.

He stared downtrail, eyes wide and looking slightly to one side as he struggled for a night-sight glimpse of the horse. Nothing. But whoever rode that horse must have seen the white canvas of the wagons. Rudge fondled his twin Colts and waited. Why hadn't he thought last night to make camp a defensible distance from those white canvas beacons? He wondered how far away their own hobbled mustangs were grazing.

"Mrs. Lowery!" It was a familiar voice but Rudge couldn't place it. He gave the owner marks for common sense.

"Who is it?" Mrs. Lowery called back.

"Sheriff Jason."

"Come in slowly, with your hands in sight." This time Rudge gave the redheaded woman marks for common sense. He heard the horse start walking again and a moment later saw the sheriff silhouetted against starlight. Rudge reversed his backward drift into the junipers and waited for the sheriff to dismount.

"That Englishman here with you?" Then the sheriff saw Rudge and nodded. There was a pause. "I'm truly sorry about all this," he finally said.

"My husband's death, or my father's?" Rudge sensed a new strain of ice in Mrs. Lowery's voice.

The sheriff was now even sorrier. Rudge felt a fleeting sympathy for the man caught in the middle. But he was not prepared to let sympathy overpower self-preservation. "Seems rather odd," Rudge said in a placating tone, "that you'd come out here all alone."

"This may turn out to be the day I earn my year's pay," the sheriff replied.

Rudge had known it would come to this sooner or later— had known it ever since he had seen that freighter hotfoot it off to the sheriff's office. Suddenly he understood Mrs. Lowery's hurry to see him out of town. He studied the sheriff, who was intelligent enough to keep his hands well away from the single Peacemaker he wore.

"Only one way in or out," the sheriff said.

Rudge wondered if someone had given him a bum steer. He had been heading this way en route to San Francisco.

"We are quite aware of our isolation!" Mrs. Lowery

snapped. "You've never seen fit to visit us before. Now why couldn't you have handled this too in your customary manner—comfortably astraddle a fence back down in Soda Springs?"

"Them's hard words, ma'am," the sheriff said. "'Specially considerin' your feelin's. Do you know what I come out here for?"

"No. Nor do I much care. You might concern yourself with the trouble you'll have proving that one man sets out deliberately to provoke hordes whose past conduct precludes any hoped defense of pacific intention."

Rudge caught himself wondering if the redheaded woman had lived among lawyers. Then he recalled she had received some schooling in the East.

Mrs. Lowery had finally broken free of the glacial restraint that had enveloped her since the loss of first a husband, then a father. "Mr. Rudge has not for one moment sat behind a desk and lectured me about the burden of proof!" she flared. "If you can't do your job, then you might have the decency to stay out of sight while somebody does it for you."

"A moment, please," Rudge interjected. He didn't want to bring up the matter right now—or any other time for that matter—but he could not in good conscience let the redhead go as far as she seemed inclined to charge out onto a shaky limb. "May I ask exactly what is the nature of the crime that requires your presence this far from the amenities of Soda Springs?"

Sheriff Jason turned to face the lesser evil. "Knew you was trouble the first time I laid eyes on you," he growled. "Should have taken you in then."

"The charge, please."

But the redheaded Mrs. Lowery was not finished. "Mr. Rudge knows the law better than I," she blazed. "Perhaps he can decide between misfeasance and malfeasance."

"I'm afraid the sheriff was thinking of charging me," Rudge said.

The sheriff turned to Mrs. Lowery. With an exaggerated patience he began, "If a lawman abuses his office that's malfeasance. If he's hemmed in by so many highbinders there ain't no way one man without any deputies can do any more than git in a lick now and then, well, that's when your *mal* turns into *mis*feasance.

"But I reckon both you and Mister Rudge know what I'm talkin' about." The graying man paused and sighed. He studied the redhead for a moment and shook his head. "Only thing puzzles me is how a smart woman like you keeps makin' the same mistake. How can you be so deadset on defendin' still another tinhorn. Now Aggie, I'm plumb ashamed of you. Red hair's no excuse—not when you and your maw come from Kansas."

"And Mr. Rudge did *not*," she said firmly. "Any tinhorn with half an ear can mimic a British accent. Mr. Rudge has demonstrated more convincing proofs of his origins."

This was the first Rudge had heard about it. He had known that women, under the obscure influences of a female temperament, often permitted themselves to fall into logically indefensible positions. But if Mrs. Lowery had taken a shine to his lanky body and his slightly shopworn charm she had by no twist of lip or glint of eye given any evidence thereto. Then he remembered that the widowed redhead had other more urgent uses for a man with two guns.

"Might work," the sheriff said thoughtfully. "It just might be enough to make that danged freighter dry up."

"If my brother will be good enough to fetch a candle and other necessaries, I'm sure Mr. Rudge will give you a deposition." She turned away from the sheriff. "By the way, Mr. Rudge, where were you in 1863?"

VIII

Rudge stared. The night was too dark to read anybody's face. "I beg your pardon?" he finally managed.

"You know danged well what she said," the sheriff growled. "Where were you in 1863?"

"I'm afraid I'd have to think for a moment."

"You've had twelve years to think."

"I've not," Rudge snapped. "I assumed you came to ask about things that happened here—within the last few days. Never fancied you might want to know whether I was in Lucknow or if I'd already gone down to join the regiment at Cawnpore."

There was a brief silence, then the sheriff said, "For a second there I could have sworn you said Quantrill."

"Where?"

"Not where. Who."

"You *do* know where Lucknow and Cawnpore are?" Mrs. Lowery asked.

"I've heard of them," the sheriff said. "Course you can't 'spect any man busy fightin' a war in this country to know all about other people's wars any more'n I can expect some Englishman off in India to know what William C. Quantrill was up to ridin' out of Missouri. It'd take somebody from Lawrence, Kansas, to remember that. Course you was kind of little, Aggie. Might not even remember your maw."

Rudge wondered why the boy had no word or suggestion throughout all this interchange. Was this quiet boy the same young rebel who had pleaded to join him? Malcolm reappeared with candle and writing implements. Rudge thanked him and scribbled a statement to the effect that he had been a lieutenant in Her Majesty's Punjab Lancers from 1862 until late in 1864, at which time he had found regimental life sufficiently boring and his indebtedness sufficiently pressing to shift allegiance to the more munificent promises of a recruiter for the Emperor's Dragoons. He signed the deposition.

Sheriff Jason found a pair of pince nez spectacles and squinted. "Emperor? Last I heerd you still had a queen over there."

"Quite right," Rudge said. "'Emperor' seems the correct English for *Kaiser*."

"You fought for the Germans?"

"For the house of Hapsburg. Kaiser Max specifically."

"Can't say I ever heard of him."

"He was doing rather nicely until his northern neighbors settled some internal conflict and once more felt the need to meddle in their neighbors' affairs."

Light burst upon the sheriff. "If I'd fought for Maximilian I wouldn't brag about it," he grunted.

"Would you be more prideful of the mischief that has plagued that unfortunate country since your meddling destroyed the last possibility for a stable government? Perhaps if everyone could foresee the consequences of his actions there might be no more wars." Rudge sighed. "In any event, what is it I am thought to have done in 1863—whilst serving in India?" He pronounced it "Injuh."

"Think I'll let Mrs. Lowery explain it," the sheriff said. He smiled and Rudge realized the old man was grateful for an out like this. Now he didn't have to try to arrest a man with a demonstrated ability to resist arrest if the mood struck him.

Jason folded Rudge's deposition, got to his feet, and tipped his hat. "See you in town the next time you have to come through," he promised, and rode off downtrail toward the thin gray band of dawn.

A night with only a blanket to separate her from the desert had done little to improve Mrs. Lowery's stiffness. While Rudge rounded up the hobbled horses, oated, watered, and harnessed them, the brooding Malcolm helped his sister start a fire. They gulped coffee, each obsessed with private thoughts and a foreboding for the heat to come.

As the light improved Rudge saw that Mrs. Lowery's color had not. She seemed finedrawn, as if recovering from a lengthy illness. He wondered if she would turn out to be of a permanently sickly nature or if she was just trying too much too soon. But as long as she asked no questions he would not pry into her silences. He helped her up onto the buckboard.

They moved out and even the mustangs seemed caught up with the obsession to cover as much trail as possible before the sun climbed all the way into another free sample of hell.

Rudge knew it was not over, that sooner or later he was going to have to sort out that business with the freighter back in Soda Springs. He tried to look on the bright side of it. Unless he changed his luck and managed, for once, to pick a winning side he would go under with the Maclendons and it would make no difference how many people might insist he looked just like—

He sighed. Hadn't slept enough last night. Now he was—not exactly sleeping, but he had managed to shift the task of driving six mustangs to some automatous corner of his mind while the remainder pondered some ideal future where every ten years a man started out afresh: new name, new profession, no memories. That was the main thing a man needed: no memories.

He jerked back into awareness. The sun was still behind, but creosote bush and paloverde had surrendered unconditionally to juniper, which, at this altitude, was midway between bush and tree. A mile ahead was a stand of those fork-topped pines he had watched the tame Indians down South harvest for an edible nut.

From his six mustangs' sudden enthusiasm he knew they must be expecting a rest in the shade ahead. It was hot and promised hotter but at this altitude the sun could never be as unendurable as at Soda Springs. He drew a deep breath and sniffed the faint but invigorating scent of *piñón*.

The buckboards were a decent, dust-settling interval ahead of his heavy wagon. By the time he reached the pines Mrs. Lowery was fixing something to eat. In the midst of the *piñones* was a tiny seep that someone had dug out and curbed with a cracker box. Malcolm had emptied their brackish canteens into the horses and was refilling them at the seep. Rudge regarded the water questioningly.

"Better'n Soda Springs," the boy reassured him.

"How much farther have we to go?"

"'Nother fifteen miles."

While the boy's sister cooked Rudge saw to the horses, tightening harness, adjusting bridles, inspecting hoofs and mouths. Despite the endless climb the mustangs were not in bad shape. He wished he could say the same for the redhead who swayed and stumbled about the fire. Mrs. Lowery was near the end of her tether. "Why don't you lie down?" he suggested. "I'll know when the corn pone's ready."

"I'm sure you will, Mr. Rudge."

He spun to study the pale, drawn woman. "You really don't know me," he said. "Why did you defend me so staunchly?"

"First things first, Mr. Rudge."

He studied the stew pot and the banked dutch oven, resisted the temptation to improve on Mrs. Lowery's arrangements.

"And after I've killed all the dragons and rescued you from the dark tower?"

"Must we discuss it now?"

"Only if you wish," Rudge said. "Is your injury bothering you much?"

"I'm afraid I have no standard for comparison."

Rudge studied the fire. He hoped Mrs. Lowery's health and disposition might improve once they reached the estate. Even under this much strain she managed to remain a very attractive woman.

"You've been a soldier," she continued. "Have you ever been wounded?"

"A few nicks and scrapes," he admitted.

"No bullet wounds?"

Rudge passed a hand over his head and felt the scab he had already knocked off once.

"How long does it take for a shoulder wound to heal?"

Rudge turned abruptly. "You've been shot? When?"

"At the time my husband was killed."

Only four or five days ago? Rudge remembered that old Maclendon's will had assumed her husband was alive. The old man hadn't thought much of his son-in-law. Was Mrs. Lowery's opinion any higher? She was pointing where the leg-of-mutton sleeve of her shirtwaist joined at the bottom. "More of a scratch than a true wound," she explained. "But it seems to open every time I move."

"You shouldn't be on the trail," Rudge said absently. "Week abed without moving and you'll be all right." He searched for some diplomatic way to inquire deeper into— To hell with diplomacy! "I seem to have involved myself inextricably in your affairs, Mrs. Lowery. Perhaps I should understand the relationship between yourself, your father, and your husband a little better."

"My husband was a wastrel," Mrs. Lowery said calmly. "Well on the road toward becoming a scoundrel."

"Oh?"

She sighed. "Had I known at sixteen all the things my father knew at fifty—" She shrugged and winced. "No doubt the sheriff was right. In some ways my husband was rather like you."

"Really, Mrs. Lowery! I can hardly offer you a choice of weapons."

"Oh, not that way, Mr. Rudge. Though the sheriff insists you are a scoundrel, I feel that your present deportment leaves nothing to be desired. I was only remembering my mother."

"I'm afraid I cannot divine the connection."

"My mother was murdered when Quantrill's guerrillas descended on Kansas. Since Lawrence was an Abolitionist town they massacred everyone."

Rudge stared.

"I have been told that war is war, that civilized behavior must needs undergo a temporary suspension. The learned often speak of the heat of battle, how violence begets violence until finally all thought of love and mercy is crowded out."

Rudge wondered how all this tied in with the way her husband had died. He wondered if she had seen him die. Must have, if she had caught a bullet too. "Was it somewhere on this trail?"

"I beg your pardon?"

"Where your husband was killed—where you were wounded."

"Oh no, Mr. Rudge. It happened in Soda Springs." She inspected the stew and cracked the lid of the dutch oven. The boy finished with the horses and brought a coffee pot from the tiny curbed spring to the fire.

"As I told you, my husband was something of a wastrel. We came to have little sympathy with one another. To lessen the scandal my father used to—" She hesitated.

"I know what a remittance man is," Rudge said.

"I found it difficult to believe that my husband would openly consort with my father's enemies," she said. "I was at a loss. I sent word several times for him to come see me but

each time brought no reply. Finally I forced myself to enter
that sinkhole where he spent his days gambling away his al-
lowance."

Rudge was beginning to see the ending of this story. He
was not particularly elated over what he saw. "There's only
one gambling hall in Soda Springs," he said.

"The Golden Eagle. My husband acquired a reputation as
a cardsharp and a bully. It was only an unhappy accident
that I happened to be coming in the back door when someone continued the argument and forced you to shoot again."

Rudge stared at Mrs. Lowery. "You've known all along it
was my bullet hit you?"

"Yes, Mr. Rudge."

"Was it I who killed your husband?"

"Yes, Mr. Rudge."

"And you're not—annoyed?"

"If you choose to live by the sword you may as well defend the Maclendons. Obviously my father saw qualities in
you that he never found in Mr. Lowery."

"But he couldn't have known—"

"My father would have been delighted, Mr. Rudge."

There was a long silence. Rudge knew better than to attempt any apology. The silent boy padded off on some errand with the horses. Rudge finally broke the silence. "Why
did he want to join me?" he demanded with a look toward
Malcolm. "Didn't your brother know I'd shot your husband
and wounded you?"

"I'm sure he did, Mr. Rudge. He was quite put out when
you forestalled his transparent little scheme."

That little bastard was planning to murder me!

"Malcolm was quite fond of my husband," she added in
that same placid tone. "Why is it, I wonder, that boys always prefer scoundrels?"

And thus, Rudge reflected, do we acquire our reputations
for sagacity. He had thought a hero-worshiping boy wanted
to join him. Instead, he must have driven both the boy and

the sheriff out of their minds trying to guess how he had
sniffed out whatever the boy had in mind for the first time
Rudge went to sleep.

"And now?"

"Now what, Mr. Rudge?"

"Now why shouldn't I preserve my precious skin by moving on before that boy fulfills his intention?"

"Slight danger of that, Mr. Rudge. I've instructed him."

"Oh?"

"In any event, my brother is rapidly shifting allegiance
from one scoundrel to another."

"You keep returning to that. Has my deportment been
less than honorable?"

"Totally honorable and totally English." There was an interruption as the boy came back and they dished up dinner.
Rudge sat beneath the *piñones* balancing a tin plate of stew
and a chunk of corn pone.

"I've noticed that you never eat bread, Mr. Rudge," the
redheaded Mrs. Lowery said. "Does everyone in England
prefer corn pone?"

IX

Rudge managed not to drop his plate. "Eckchooly—" he laid it on with a trowel while he sought for some believable explanation. "Corn in England is what you call wheat, barley, rye, or any other grain. What you Americans call corn is known to us as maize, or sometimes Indian corn."

"But do you eat it?"

"I've heard that the poorer classes do on occasion. There was some scandal about poisoning the Irish with it during the last famine." He drew a breath and continued, "But in Mexico one finds little else to eat.

"Wheat does not flourish in the tropics and the natives have little taste for expensive imports. In time one surrenders to the inevitability of corn *tortillas*, corn *tamales*, corn *sopes*, corn *menudo*, corn everything. The native religion has several tutelary deities for the maize plant."

"And were you long in Mexico?"

"Until 1867."

"Oh? What caused you to leave?"

Rudge sighed. "At sunrise on the nineteenth of June, on a small hill outside of Querétaro a firing squad put an end to Hapsburg hopes, thus ending a period of relative stability and prosperity."

The red-haired Mrs. Lowery's Yankee face was turning dangerous but Rudge pressed on. "It was a peaceable country," he insisted, "with every hope for a government with some continuity—until hostilities ceased in this country and the Yankees were once more free to meddle."

"But Juárez was a national hero!" Mrs. Lowery sputtered.

"It's difficult to reconcile patriotism with an offer to sell Lower California."

"Really, Mr. Rudge!"

"An offer refused by you Americans only because of some haggling over whether the territory would be brought in as a free—or as a slave state.

"Failing in this, the national hero offered to sell a railroad right-of-way from Brownsville to Mazatlán which, in the natural course of events, would have halved his already diminished country."

"I find this difficult to believe, Mr. Rudge."

"The documents are of public record. Will you believe your own newspapers of a decade ago? In any event, Juárez had local competition quite apart from the emperor. General Díaz is also a great patriot, who lost no opportunity for mischief while Juárez lived. When Díaz lost the election some five years ago he immediately started a rebellion. At the height of it Juárez conveniently died. It was only then that General Díaz found it expedient to worship publicly at the tomb of a national hero—once his rival was safely dead.

"I'm sure the general manages to smile behind his tears since Juárez also offered the Yankees a land route across the Isthmus—which would have connected the two oceans at the expense of the general's home state. Oddly enough, also the home state of Juárez."

Mrs. Lowery's eyes were beginning to glaze. Her brother's expression was unfathomable.

"The only extenuation for Señor Juárez' efforts to peddle his country piecemeal was his desperate position. The emperor's forces had reduced him to the status of a petty bandit. Though forced to hide in New Orleans, he got no arms as long as the *gringos* were busy murdering one another. It was only when your war ended that diplomatic pressure in Europe, plus arms to spare at home, changed the situation and Juárez triumphed.

"And thus General Díaz found himself in the embarrassing position of having been in open revolt against a national hero. His only solution was to lay wreaths on the hero's tomb and water them liberally with his tears.

"I leave it to you to decide what kind of hero Señor Juárez would have been, had he succeeded in selling Baja California, all of the mainland north of a line from Brownsville to Mazatlán, and everything south of the Isthmus: the national hero and preserver of a remnant the approximate size of Massachusetts."

"You feel strongly on the subject, Mr. Rudge."

"One prefers not to lose. What annoys me most is the vilification of the emperor. It's all very well to speak of democracy—which the Greeks found unworkable. Have you re-established popular government in your unhappy southern neighbor? Or have you allowed every freebooter to carve out his fiefdom? The only losers are those l umble citizens who never sought a vote, were too uneducated to exercise it, who wished only to live in peace and without fear of brigands."

"But an emperor—" the redhead protested.

"God save the Queen!" Rudge snapped. "Preserve her in comfort and wealth. Spare us the sight of new and ever more greedy rascals with each election."

Wordlessly, Mrs. Lowery poured coffee. Rudge gave an inward sigh of relief. But he knew this was not the end of it. They finished their meal in silence. He had thought a little argument would restore some life to the wan redhead but Mrs. Lowery remained pale and silent. "You're going to have to lie down for a while," Rudge said. "Recruit your strength."

"I'm quite capable—"

"You are not. If you don't try to rest I may be obliged to practice medicine. Quite apart from my questionable abilities, to dress your wound will require undressing you."

Mrs. Lowery turned nearly as red as her hair but she lay down while Rudge and Malcolm washed up and put away.

"How's the road from here on?" Rudge asked.

"Tolerable," the boy grumped.

"Is it any better than behind us?"

"'Bout the same."

"Your sister worries me."

"She worries lots of people."

Rudge qualified his remark. "She's more ill than she lets on. Don't you want her to live?"

The boy's reserve abruptly evaporated. "You ain't funnin' me?"

Rudge assured the boy that he was not. "You seem reasonably knowledgeable. Will the road permit hitching one buckboard behind my wagon?"

"So Aggie can lay down?"

"So Aggie can lie down."

It was near noon before they had made the necessary adaptations in harness to hitch still another pair of mustangs to Rudge's wagon and lash the tongue of the buckboard to the junction of the heavier wagon's rear axle and perch.

Rudge reshuffled his load into some semblance of levelness and stuffed feedbags into the gaps. He helped Mrs. Lowery into the wagon, mildly surprised at how little she weighed. "You'll be all right now?" he asked. "Anything you need before we start moving?"

"Only my rifle."

The boy found the heavy piece in her buckboard and handed it up. Rudge took the lead this time so the boy could keep an eye on the trailing buckboard. They exited the *piñon* grove and the sun began extracting interest for the time they had managed to stay out of it. He glanced over his shoulder to see how Mrs. Lowery was taking the unsprung freight wagon's progress from rock to rut. The pale woman was either sleeping already or she had fainted. Now what was he going to do if she were to up and die on him?

Shouldn't have pounded on her Yankee sensibilities with all that monarchist malarkey, he guessed. But it was a necessary part of any Yankee's education to see those viewpoints their schools preferred to ignore. And Rudge's counterattack had served its immediate purpose. If only Sheriff Jason were that easy to humbug . . .

He'd had his hands full with six horses. Now he was struggling to control eight of the brutes, swinging wide on each turn to keep the trailing, corner-cutting buckboard from overturning. All he needed was another encounter with bandits—another runaway.

But despite the continual climb the horses' cheerfulness improved as the countryside greened. The desert was behind now, supplanted by the thin western forests of aspen, interspersed with stands of *piñón*, sugar pine, and an occasional droopy-limbed tamarack. The grass was thick but well eaten over. Rudge had never seen grass cropped that close before. He glanced back but Mrs. Lowery was still asleep.

Time enough to see for himself what bucktoothed breed of cattle the Maclendons ran in this sparse country. He tried to remember what month it was. Late May, he guessed. If the graze was like this now, what would cattle feed on come September? This, no doubt, was at least one of the reasons for all the shooting.

An hour passed and still no sign of life. Up ahead he could see the mountains rising into snowcapped peaks. Somewhere up there would be green and watered valleys where the grass would last throughout the summer—providing deer and antelope did not get it all first. But as Rudge jounced his double rig over the ruts he wondered. There was not the slightest circular sign that any cow had ever plopped on this closecropped grass. The country was clean as the park of some country estate in Buckinghamshire.

The road passed through a stand of sugar pine and something large and black hurtled past like a spent cannon ball. Rudge had his pistols out before he realized it was only a flying squirrel. Overhead a whiskey jack evicted a crow, then the grove was silent again save for the snorting and constant flatulation of his eight mustangs. He recaptured reins and sorted them out before disaster could overtake the double rig.

The boy had said fifteen miles. Surely they had covered over half of that. The horses were trotting as if pasture and freedom lay just around the next bend. But when he rounded the next bend there was nothing but a wagon rather like the Gypsy caravans he had seen in parts of England.

The wagon lay on its side. Smoke still rose from smoldering shreds of canvas over the cracked bows. Rudge stood on the seat and hauled on eight sets of reins until he had managed to halt the team. He set the brake on the wagon, jumped down, and went back to inspect the shattered caravan. A man lay on the far side. He was old and looked either Mexican or Indian. He would never grow any older.

"Arcadio!" The boy had tied his buckboard and come up to join Rudge.

"One of yours?"

The boy nodded.

The old man had been shot. The bullet had shattered his right arm and gone on to drag bone splinters somewhere into the middle of his chest. There was a great deal of blood. Rudge watched from the corner of his eye to see if young Malcolm was used to the sight of messy and unromantic death. If the younger Maclendon was perturbed he did a magnificent job of concealing it as he went back to his buckboard for a tarp.

Between them Rudge and the boy got the stiffening body into the boy's buckboard. "Anything you'd like to save from the caravan?" Rudge asked.

"The what?"

"The wagon."

"Oh." The boy hesitated for a moment, then crawled into the overturned wagon. In a moment he emerged with a crudely carved crucifix and one of those garish pictures Rudge had seen as *ex voto* offerings in the churches down South. Malcolm seemed slightly embarrassed to hold these relics of idolatry in his Protestant hands. "*Retablo*," he explained. "Means a lot to his family."

"Probably not as much as would the old man alive," Rudge guessed. He put a shoulder to the capsized caravan and with the boy's help they got it far enough off the trail to pass. "Much farther?" he asked.

"'Nother three or four miles," the boy said.

Rudge repeated the business of loosening the buckboard brake, then his larger wagon's. He glanced worriedly at the comatose Mrs. Lowery before sorting out reins and urging the eight mustangs to try at least to start out together.

He supposed he ought to have figured it out long ago. One simple question back down in Soda Springs would have removed all the mystery. But he had been too careful, too unwilling to put himself under any obligation to the local citizenry. And now here he was sixty miles and eight thousand feet from town, freighting into a ranch that boasted some ten thousand head. A ranch without a brand. No wonder the Maclendons were not popular.

The old man whose life he had tried to save—Maclendon could have told him. They could all have told him. "*Tell them it's Maclendon!*" The old Scotsman had prided himself on his ability to get on with the Indians. Old Maclendon had been here first. And a lot of good it had done him. People in this country were reasonably tolerant of some things. They didn't go out of their way to ask embarrassing questions unless a stranger made himself conspicuous the way Rudge had.

These people were descended of misfits and troublemakers. They would forgive and forget, were not inclined to visit the sins of the father onto generations of sons. Might even be inclined to forgive Maclendon his lack of a registered brand. But there was one sin no cattleman would abide.

"Ten thousand head and get," Rudge muttered.

"I beg your pardon?" Mrs. Lowery had finally awakened again.

"Ten thousand head and get," he repeated.

"Possibly. But I fear there may be less by now. That tally was before all the trouble started."

"How long has it been going on?"

"A few months."

"Never any trouble before that?"

"None," Mrs. Lowery said. "Not until others began trying to run cattle on our range."

Rudge growled something unintelligible.

"You seem angry, Mr. Rudge. Did something happen while I slept?"

"Several things, Mrs. Lowery, but I'm afraid my annoyance is directed mostly at myself."

"Oh?"

"The framework of human society is mutual trust," he said. "Falsehood annoys us only because it is the exception to the rule."

Mrs. Lowery found no grounds for disagreement.

"But confound it!" Rudge snarled, "someone might have told me those ten thousand head were *sheep!*"

X

"Don't they run sheep in England?" Mrs. Lowery asked.

"A great many," Rudge admitted. "America might still be totally Spanish, had it not been profitable a century ago to transport all the tenant farmers over here to make room for sheep at home."

"You are opposed to sheep?"

"My preferences are of slight import. Do you truly believe that I am totally devoid of any instinct for self-preservation?" Rudge demanded. "Were I to look upon sheep with the same joy that Jehovah found in Abel's offering, it would do me small good in a land where we are outnumbered by the irate sons of Cain." He paused and added, "Even mercenaries hesitate to die for a cause that is totally without merit."

"Without merit, Mr. Rudge? What clothing do you wear? Do you sleep under cotton?"

"No need to convince me," Rudge growled. "Convince your *bull*headed neighbors that sheep do not destroy grass, foul the water, and constitute an abomination in the sight of a cow-loving god."

"Does it mean nothing that we were here first?"

"Before the Indians?"

"My father made his peace with them. Until recently there was room for all."

Rudge's nose told him they must be nearing the estate. He held his tongue in hopes the woman behind him would do likewise. There was a faint whisper of breeze and the smell was suddenly stronger.

He recalled a professor of Natural Philosophy whose ideas had made him the butt of countless student pranks. The old man had insisted against all common sense that smells went deeper into a man's soul than things seen or heard. This was not sheep. It was something Rudge wished he could forget. Knowing what he was about to find, he also wished he had been less abrasive with the poor woman who lay behind him. But suddenly she was clambering out to sit on the box beside him. She looked at Rudge. "I'm afraid so," he said.

The wagon topped a slight rise and the estate grounds were in view ahead. Rudge sighed and found no joy in seeing he had been right.

Tiny tendrils of smoke still rose from the ashes that had once been house, stable, all the various outbuildings. At the far edge of the clearing a bundle of rags poked dispiritedly through a small ring of ashes, raking them apart with a leafy branch. The old woman looked up, startled by the noise of the horses, and recognized Mrs. Lowery. She emitted a shrill wail and stumbled toward them.

Rudge halted the eight mustangs and helped Mrs. Lowery down. The women fell over one another and Rudge noted that the redhead's Spanish, though fluent, bore unmistakable overtones of Ayrshire.

Malcolm halted his buckboard and seemed too overwhelmed to move. Rudge remembered when he had returned to a ruined estate and scattered family. He busied himself unhitching and hobbling the mustangs and gave the surviving Maclendons time to collect themselves.

It was a well-chosen site for a ranch. There were aspens on one side of the tiny creek and sugar pines across the meadow. The hollow's only defect was that it was indefensible. Anyone could shoot down into it from either side. The old man must have been sure of the Indians, Rudge guessed, or he would never have picked this dell for his headquarters.

He had the mustangs unhitched, unharnessed, and hobbled and still the boy, his sister, and the old woman huddled together.

Rudge unhitched the team from the boy's buckboard and began rooting out camping gear. He wondered how long since the old woman had eaten.

"*Ayer*," he heard her say, which meant yesterday. Since smoke still rose here and there he supposed she meant the burnout. He scraped embers from what must once have been the great house and piled charred ends of boards until he had a fire going. Supper was well underway before the trio recovered enough to join him.

"*¿Algunos muertos?*" he asked the old woman. And asking her if there were any dead reminded him of the old man wrapped in a tarp in the boy's buckboard. He glanced at Malcolm who obviously had also forgotten. "Hers?"

The boy nodded.

Rudge considered another outburst of grief and took the coward's way out. "Watch out supper doesn't burn," he told the redhead and left her and Malcolm to break the news. He poked through the buckboard and found a shovel. Behind the ring of ashes he found a tiny graveyard. He picked a clear spot and began digging. Back by the fire a fresh round of wailing told him someone else had done the dirty work.

The old woman wanted a proper *velorio* but Rudge convinced her that without a priest or a Catholic quorum there was little point in an all-night wake. "God needs no one to tell him your husband was a good man," he explained, not mentioning that no amount of goodness could counteract the old man's having already lain a whole day in the sun.

It was over. Darkness had fallen and they ate a half-dried-out supper by the unwavering light of a candle. "And how are you feeling now, Mrs. Lowery?"

She sighed.

"I'm sorry, Mr. Rudge."

"For what?"

"For dragging you into our troubles."

Rudge was too tired to make up polite lies. "Tomorrow," he said. "Malcolm, do you feel up to standing first watch?"

"Reckon I can," the boy said.

Rudge rolled up in his blanket and tried to turn himself off. Despite his exhaustion it was not easy. Ten thousand head—even of sheep—must have required a goodly number of herders. Where were they? Where were the sheep? Tomorrow he would have to ask the old woman.

He awoke struggling. Somebody was trying to smother him. Then he saw it was Mrs. Lowery. He pulled her hands away. "What is it?" he whispered.

Mrs. Lowery's face approached his ear and he caught a faint scent of lavender. "Somebody's coming," she whispered.

He got into his boots and pistols and oozed away into the brush. Malcolm and Mrs. Lowery got the old woman on her feet and they scooted off in another direction. Rudge waited. Suddenly he knew it was a false alarm. "¿Quién?" he called.

"Eusebio." It was a soft, Spanish voice. They reassembled in the darkness and Rudge waited to see who it would turn out to be. One thing was obvious: no cowboy's horse would wear a sheep bell.

Eusebio was a dark-skinned, middle-aged man with a wispy Mandarin mustache and abundant black hair to his shoulders. Though he probably weighed twice as much, he stood a head shorter than Rudge. The unsuspecting Eusebio's sheep were fattening well and when last he had been here the Maclendons had been at peace with their neighbors and their gods. But his sheep were running low on salt so he had come down—to this.

He wandered dazedly through the starlight, unable to believe the destruction that surrounded him, even when the old woman dogged his steps with a detailed recital. It took Rudge some time to understand that the middle-aged Eusebio must be either son or nephew to the new widow.

"*¿Y no le ha molestado nadie allá arriba?*" Rudge asked when finally they squatted nursing coffee by the fire.

"Nobody bother me up there." Eusebio's English was as good as Rudge's Spanish. "Sheep all in box *cañón*. Be fine for couple days. This been a good year. No wolf, no coyote, no—" His English finally gave out. "*¿Trotona?*"

"Scrapie," the redhead offered. When Rudge still didn't understand she elaborated. "The poor beasts go mad from an itch. They scrape the wool and hide off their backs until finally they die."

Rudge wondered what idiot had assumed that God tempers the wind to the shorn lamb. "Is there no cure?"

"Kill sick ones," Eusebio said. "Kill five years now. This year sheep look pretty good."

The talk wound down and finally they all went back to sleep, save Rudge who sat wrapped in his blanket waiting for the dawn and realizing with a certain rue that he was reaching an age where coffee in the middle of the night did not lie that well on his stomach. He tried to comfort himself with the thought that at least he was not a sheep, did not have scrapie. He tried to sort out what had happened.

Seemed straightforward enough. The Maclendons had come into this country, had made their peace with the Indians, and had prospered—until the country opened up and other lesser breeds had decided this land was too good for sheep, too good for Maclendons who perhaps bore the same odor. Once the others were awake again he would have to find out how many head in Eusebio's herd, how many other herders, and what chance the other herds might have remained as unmolested as Eusebio's.

He had heard before about the eternal threeway competition between cow, sheep, and farmer. In this country, so far at least, the farmers were not a significant faction. Usually in these wars of attrition cattle and sheep men stampeded each other's herds over the nearest cliff or used whatever was handy to make the other's business unprofitable. But here the newcomers were not beating around the bush. They weren't killing Maclendon sheep. They were killing Maclendons.

Rosy-fingered dawn came to a red-eyed Rudge. He checked his Colts, went down to the tiny creek to make his toilet. By the time he returned, the others were awake. Mrs. Lowery seemed somewhat recovered but she was still far from well. "Any proud flesh?" Rudge asked.

"No, Mr. Rudge." She seemed worried by this lack.

"There is a new school of thought in London and Edinburgh," he said. "Sir Joseph Lister believes pus is the first step toward mortification. He says wounds heal best without such infection."

"How odd."

"Yes, isn't it?" Rudge was bitter. He remembered all those nicks in hand or foot that surgeons had routinely treated by amputation at the next joint and, a week later, at the next joint above that since nobody had the time or inclination to boil his tools between victims. How many centuries would it take for the latest word to travel from London to America? "But in your case," he comforted her, "recruitment should be swift if you'll just try not to move for a few days."

"Yes," she said absently. "Perhaps *I* shall recruit my health." She looked around the wasted ranch.

"Are you and Malcolm the only Maclendons?"

She nodded.

"Then I'm afraid you'll have to come to some decision."

"Decision, Mr. Rudge?"

"You can gather the remains of your property and drive them to market while there's still something left to save."

"And give up?" As the red-haired Mrs. Lowery's eyes burned into Rudge he abruptly realized this was one possibility that had never occurred to her. There was a moment's silence, then she added, "It's different for you, Mr. Rudge. You've no stake or roots in this country. I'm sorry to have involved you so deeply in our affairs. Tell me how much we owe you and I'll give you a draft on our bank and you'll be free of us."

Rudge bowed. "Nothing, Mrs. Lowery. To the contrary, I'm indebted to you."

The redhead did not understand.

He was overcome by a sudden suspicion. "Did they perchance call your husband Doc?"

"No, Mr. Rudge."

"Then I fear your husband was as much a victim as I. When it became obvious that the gentleman known as Doc was dealing cards with a total disregard for the laws of chance he tried to shift the blame by dealing winning cards to me. It took all my skill to shift them back. The result—" He shrugged. "You were there."

"I'm afraid I still don't understand, Mr. Rudge."

"It's difficult to say where the money would have ended up in an honest game. But I suspect it originated in sheep. I dislike being called a tinhorn. Will you accept the thousand dollars I won?"

"No, Mr. Rudge. But I shall gratefully accept your services in like amount."

Rudge knew he had been outmaneuvered. But the redhaired Mrs. Lowery was no longer the wan ghost of moments ago. "Now lie back and be still," he ordered. "I'm going to look about and see what can be salvaged."

Malcolm and Eusebio joined him for a tour of the ashes. The forge and smithy tools would be usable once the hammers had new handles. A few iron and clay pots survived in the ashes of the kitchen. Elsewhere a pair of brass bedsteads had fused nearly beyond recognition. There was not the slightest sooty remnant of anything that could be eaten by man, horse, or sheep. "How many people normally lived about the great house?" he asked.

"Hard tellin'," Malcolm offered. "Some times of year there'd be twenty or thirty people. Other times only three or four."

Rudge remembered the payroll he had gone over down in Soda Springs, with all those DB, death benefit abbreviations, he had mistaken for debits. The cattlemen must have been bushwhacking herders for some time. They wandered aimlessly around the clearing kicking at ashes, and he knew what was in the back of everybody's mind: what was the use of rebuilding if they could not defend this spot, if their neighbors would just come to burn them out again?

"How far is the—" What had they called that penny-farthing bicycle brand?

"Oostenveld?"

"Are they the nearest?"

"Nearest and biggest. They're about fifteen miles downstream."

"Downstream?" Rudge's ears pricked up.

Malcolm and Eusebio assured him that he had heard correctly.

"I wonder what might happen to people downstream if we were to divert this creek?"

There was a moment of startled silence, then Malcolm gave a bitter laugh. "Sure save us the trouble of lookin' for them!"

"They be up here damn quick," Eusebio added. "Ain' no more water this side of slope!"

"Now where," Rudge asked, "would there be a likely spot for diversion?"

XI

Their enthusiasm evaporated as suddenly as it had come.

Rudge knew that mountain streams usually had deep watercourses, that any canyons would branch the wrong way, flowing into this valley instead of out. But he might as well look around.

"Has anyone ever threatened something like this?" he asked. Maybe the people downstream had other things on their minds besides the smell of sheep.

If old Maclendon had ever put this kind of a scare into the ○ ○ brand neither Malcolm nor Eusebio had heard about it. Rudge made a mental note to ask Mrs. Lowery. He strolled downstream trying to remember what the country had looked like when he had driven the wagon up into here. But his mind had been on other things, like keeping eight mustangs in line. Lost in his own thoughts, he lagged while Malcolm and Eusebio pressed ahead chattering in the rapid and oddly accented Spanish of this mountain region.

"*¡Señor Rawtch!*"

Rudge had observed that Latins can seldom hear the murky shadings of a tongue evolved where sunlight is as scarce as an open-mouthed vowel. "*Para mis amigos es Bentley,*" he suggested, then he saw what had excited them. Malcolm and Eusebio were looking at a fresh grave. The mound of dirt could not be over a day or two old. It lay within a dozen paces of the creek.

"Who is it?" Malcolm wondered.

Eusebio studied the mound forebodingly.

Rudge remembered how the murderers had left the old

man—Eusebio's father or uncle—sprawled beside a burnt-out caravan. Why would they have buried somebody here? "You might look in on your sister as you're bringing a shovel," he suggested to Malcolm.

"You're gonna dig it up?"

"Unless you can devise some easier way to find out." He turned to Eusebio. "I fancy there's not the slightest hope of a priest within a hundred miles?"

The thickset herder assured him that there was not. He seemed unusually bitter over this lack. Rudge offered him a cheroot and they sat smoking by the creek waiting for the boy to come back with the shovel. "Where you learn Spanish?"

"Down South."

"¡Cabrones!"

Rudge raised his eyebrows. "You don't like the people down there?"

Eusebio spat. "Goddamn revolutions. You think I care what they do in Mexico? You think I'm Mexican?"

Rudge had assumed as much.

"My people from Spain. We live three hundred years this place. Son of a bitch down South wants revolution, tha's fine. Me, I don' start no revolution. Spanish army, priest—all go. Leave me fight Indians. Americans come this country, tha's good. Mexicans come talk revolution, hell wit' them. 'Nough trouble wit' Indians."

"Are you still having Indian trouble?"

"Not so bad now. Señor Maclendon treat 'em pretty good."

It was reassuring to have a second opinion. Rudge was ready to ask more questions when Malcolm came trotting back with the shovel. Rudge took first turn at digging.

The dirt was soft and easily removed. He had scooped out a foot of it before the boy jumped down to replace him. Ten minutes later they had scooped out three feet of loose soil and Rudge was increasingly puzzled. A grave was odd enough. Would bushwhackers with no regard for life and property bother to dig a regulation six feet? Why would they dig a grave at all? "You're sure you've no idea who might be buried here?" he asked.

They did not. There were so many people missing that it could be anybody. Abruptly Rudge knew who it had to be. Bushwhackers wouldn't waste time burying a victim. But they might do the honors for one of their own. Still he puzzled. Bury one of their own here? Why not take him home? It just didn't make sense. He jumped down into the hole to spell Eusebio with the shovel.

Soon the short thickset herder could not see out of the hole. Rudge helped him out and began digging again. He had not gone six inches before he struck hardpan. He scraped the dirt carefully away and finally convinced himself that the ground beneath him was undisturbed. They had dug more than six feet down and the grave was empty.

Eusebio shrugged. "They bury somebody, why they dig up again?"

It was beyond Rudge. He wiped his face and lit another cheroot. Thoughtfully, they returned to the makeshift camp. "I believe our first move," he told Mrs. Lowery, "should be away from here."

"I'm not giving up!"

"Nor I," Rudge said. "But this place cannot be defended. I recommend a move up or downstream until we find some spot less susceptible to surprise."

She gave in, leaving Rudge to wonder just what he could do. He nodded toward the boy and Eusebio, who were seeing to the horses. "The herder seems an able man. Will he fight for you?"

"I couldn't say, Mr. Rudge. But he must have little love for those who killed his father and burned down his house."

"How able is your brother?"

"How able is any untried man?"

Rudge sighed. "For you to fire a rifle will surely open that wound again."

"I see what you're getting at," the redhead said. "But if we sit here and wait for them—"

"I cannot leave you defenseless. Too bad you couldn't have stayed in town."

"I saw no safety in Soda Springs."

Rudge sighed. It was beginning to look as if the Maclendons didn't have a friend in the world.

"Eusebio cannot stay much longer," she added. "Another day and his sheep will have scattered until it would take all summer to round up those the wolves did not find first."

"How many guns with the penny-farthings?"

Mrs. Lowery did not know. "For the few cattle they run, entirely too many," she guessed.

"I wonder if there's the faintest possibility that someone else is involved."

"Of course. The ○o brand is the largest but there are at least three or four smaller outfits have grabbed off pieces of our land downstream."

"Your land?"

"Call it what you will, Mr. Rudge. We Maclendons came first."

"Have you ever—expressed your displeasure?"

"The downstream land was never that important. For cows, perhaps. But sheep are a hardier animal. They follow the melting snow."

Rudge nodded and took another restless turn around the ruined ranch. He remembered how few people had turned out for old Maclendon's funeral. Obviously, the old man had thought himself more important than others did. Had he put on airs like some *grand seigneur* and rubbed these plain folk the wrong way?

But that could wait. Somebody—it had to be that penny-farthing Oostenveld brand—seemed intent on wiping out the last Maclendon. Once it became known that Rudge was allied with the clan Maclendon . . . But then, he had already exchanged lead with the penny-farthings. There was no turning back.

Ten thousand head and get. A sheep must be worth at least a dollar. What was he to do for one third of—? There was but one way to do it. He was outnumbered and even the most elementary military text admits that the smaller force gains nothing by waiting. He caught and saddled one of the mustangs and spurred it to the hilltop. From up here he could see most of the country for a mile up and downstream. No surprises on the way, he decided.

The hilltop was a quarter mile from the creek and flat enough for a camp. He went back down and considered the freight wagon. Too heavy. He got Malcolm and Eusebio to unloading one of the buckboards.

Finally, he got eight sweating horses to move half a load uphill. It was past noon before their entire lot of supplies was on the hilltop, two buckboards upended, with barrels and sacks piled in the open ends of their "fort." He sent the boy downhill to chop poles for a tarpaulin shade.

The old woman, whose name he still did not know, made it under her own power. So would Mrs. Lowery if Rudge had not offered to turn abusive. To bounce her uphill on a buckboard would be as damaging as for her to walk it. Finally he and Eusebio made a chair of their arms and carried a furiously blushing Mrs. Lowery between them.

"*No pesa nada*," the shepherd said worriedly as they went downhill to pick up odds and ends.

"Oh, she weighs *something*," Rudge said. "But admittedly not enough. Can you—?" He remembered Mrs. Lowery's warning about scattered sheep and changed his mind about asking Eusebio to stay the night. Instead, he helped him load a packhorse with salt and head back up toward the high pasture. "You have used your rifle against people?" he asked.

"Indians," Eusebio said.

"Have care. This time it will not be Indians."

The herder nodded. He was mounting his horse when he changed his mind and got down long enough to remove the sheep bell.

Rudge watched him ride up the creek and out of sight, then turned to help Malcolm who was struggling to lash a bundle of poles travois-fashion to a mustang who was not all that taken with the idea. They had just about convinced the beast to co-operate when he heard a faint whistle. It was from the hilltop. The old woman was waving a rag.

Rudge sprang onto his mount and charged uphill.

"*Allí abajo*," the old woman said.

Rudge looked *down there*. "Fancy that," he murmured.

Two men were riding up the creek, following the same path he had taken with the wagons. He studied them, wishing for a spyglass. But it was not really necessary. They rode the small mustangs of this country but both were large men. Both wore "city" clothes. Both had booted carbines. He could see no sign of pistol about either man. They were making no effort to conceal themselves. "Know them?" he asked the redhead.

Mrs. Lowery did not.

Malcolm came uphill with the load of poles. The strangers were still downstream from the burnt-out ranch. Rudge watched as they came in sight of the ashes. Even at this distance it was obvious that neither man had been expecting this. Their horses drew together and the men talked for a moment, then one looked up and saw the improvised hilltop fort.

"Mr. Lowery?" His voice came thinly up to where Rudge and the others waited. Rudge stood and waved. The strangers began urging their tired horses uphill. "Mr. Lowery?" one repeated.

"I'm afraid not," Rudge admitted. "But perhaps you could deal with Mrs. Lowery."

They were, unless Rudge had lost his eye for detail, somehow connected with money. Not big, railroad-style money. He studied their carefully inconspicuous affluence and decided these men were bankers. Now how had the word gotten out so quickly?

The one who had spoken glanced down at the burnt-out ranch. "Indians?" he asked. "They told me this country was safe."

"This lot of barbarians wears hats," Rudge said. He turned to the redhead who lay on a makeshift couch, half-covered with a blanket. "Mrs. Lowery."

The banker tipped his hat. "Alexander Tedrow," he said. "No doubt you're cognizant of Mr. Lowery's affairs?"

"Only partly."

Tedrow paused. Both men were still shaken by the mass of ashes down by the creek. "You're ill," Tedrow managed. "Have we come at an inconvenient time?"

Tedrow had a look of comforting stability about him. He would be a Mason or an Oddfellow, Rudge decided, would limit himself to two drinks per day, and his neighbors would make certain that he sat on committees for the new school or whatever. The man who accompanied Tedrow was younger and though he dressed just as conservatively, showed too much white of eye for Rudge to feel relaxed in his presence.

The younger man was staring at Rudge with a puzzled look. "Haven't we met somewhere?" he asked.

"It's a small world," Rudge said in his best London enunciation. "All things are possible."

"Guess not," the wide-eyed man decided.

There was an awkward pause and the old woman muttered something Rudge didn't catch.

"Are you, uh—empowered to act in Mr. Lowery's behalf?" Tedrow asked.

"I'm not," Rudge said. "You'll have to talk to her."

The banker was embarrassed. "I'm afraid the law would not permit—"

"I'm sure it would not," the redhead said. "The law permits a spendthrift to squander his wife's property but turns helpless whenever a wife tries to see to her own interests."

"We live in an imperfect world," Tedrow began.

"But also a world which has moved one tiny step closer toward perfection," Rudge said. "Mrs. Lowery is not a wife. She is a widow."

The bankers stared at one another and the wide-eyed man's eyes grew more haunted. "Well," Tedrow shrugged. "It's been a long ride from Santa Fe and I suppose it'll be just as long and profitless a ride back." He turned back to Mrs. Lowery. "Unless you'd care to follow through with Mr. Lowery's deal. Same terms."

"I have yet to hear what the deal is."

"Mr. Lowery offered to sell the ranch. We are prepared to offer twenty thousand dollars."

XII

Mrs. Lowery glanced at Rudge. His first reaction was to tell her to take the money and run. Then he abruptly realized what was wrong. At the same moment the redhead's face changed and he knew she had seen it too. Poor woman! That scoundrel had been her husband.

"Do you have anything with his signature on it?" Rudge asked.

Tedrow rummaged through a coat pocket and extracted a small portfolio. He handed Rudge a letter. Rudge studied the handwriting—which he had never seen before. If it was genuine the letter was straightforward enough:

Soda Springs, N. Mex.

Dear Mr. Tedrow,   *April 3, 1875*

> *Things look even better. If you still want it you can have the whole place for $25,000.*

Yrs. truly,

J. Lowery

Wordlessly, Rudge handed the letter to Mrs. Lowery.

She read it stony-faced. "I'm afraid there's been some mistake," she said. "This ranch is my father's. Mr. Lowery had no claim."

"There's five thousand dollars between your offer and Lowery's price," Rudge added.

"There's always a difference between asking and buying

prices," Tedrow said. "In any event, if the sale is off we may as well cover what ground we can back toward civilization."

"Do you have any use for that letter?" Rudge asked.

The banker shrugged. "Do you?"

"There may well be some lawsuits in the local courts," Rudge explained. "It could prove useful."

Tedrow glanced at his partner who seemed less happy with this turn of events. He glanced skyward, saw no aid forthcoming, and surrendered. "Might as well let him have it."

Rudge thanked them for the letter. Mrs. Lowery asked if they cared to spend the night. Tedrow gave a nervous glance at the fortified air of the camp and asked, "You're sure there won't be Indians on the trail?"

"Not Indians," Rudge reassured him. "But watch out for our neighbors downstream."

The bankers tipped their hats, mounted, and urged their horses back downhill. The Maclendons and the old woman watched them disappear. Rudge studied the letter again and sighed. "It *is* your husband's hand, is it not?" he asked.

"I'm afraid it is, Mr. Rudge."

"I'm sorry."

"What're *you* sorry about?" Malcolm grumped.

Rudge studied the boy. He looked back to Mrs. Lowery, suddenly wondering if perhaps she didn't understand either.

"Why did you ask for the letter, Mr. Rudge?"

Wordlessly, he pointed at the date.

"Oh!" Suddenly the slightly built woman seemed even smaller.

"What is it?" the boy demanded.

"Mr. Lowery was offering a ranch he could only sell after your sister inherited. April third was three weeks before I found your father still alive."

The boy's face abruptly changed. He turned and walked away. Rudge remembered the redhead's remark. Why was it, he wondered, that the sober, honest people who hold the world together have no fascination for boys? Why do young hero-worshipers always fix their affections on scoundrels? Poor Malcolm! First Rudge had killed his hero. Now Rudge had exposed his hero's probable role in bushwhacking his father.

"I'm afraid Mr. Tedrow was right," Mrs. Lowery said.

"In what way?"

"We live in a less than perfect world."

Rudge knew there was little to be gained by vilifying a man he had killed. "I'd better see to the horses," he said. "Wouldn't want anyone to leave us afoot." He gave the country a final look over and went down to capture four of the hobbled beasts who grazed below. By the time he returned, the boy had recovered and once more sat glumly beside his sister.

The boy was entirely too silent. Rudge remembered the boy's eagerness that first morning when he had begged to join him. He suspected that no matter how postmortems might rearrange the facts, that morning, when the boy had still not known his father was dead . . . But who could say what went on inside a seventeen-year-old's mind? Rudge could scarcely remember the burning issues that had driven him forth to alter an immutable world.

But here he was still trying to alter it after all these years. He made a firm resolve that once he had gotten Mrs. Lowery back on her feet and established some equilibrium in this country, he would shake the dust of it from his boots and see what lay ahead in San Francisco. This was no place for a man of his leanings to settle down. Sheep, for God's sake!

"Maybe I should have accepted their offer." It was Mrs. Lowery.

"Perhaps," Rudge said absently. "Maybe your husband saw this coming and had your best interests at heart after all."

"Thank you for trying," she said. "But good intentions could never have predicted my father's death."

The old woman began building a fire and putting together a meal. They watched in silence as she added chiles and onions to a piece of stringy mutton. Rudge suspected this stew was going to prove hotter than anything he had ever eaten down South. Instead of the usual corn tortillas, the old woman made a wheat-flour dough, which she rolled thin and sliced into triangles. The triangles fluffed into tiny pillows as she fried them. "¿Y esos?" Rudge asked.

"Sopapillas," the old woman explained.

For the first time Rudge realized that Eusebio was probably right. These people had survived alone in these mountains since long before New Spain had taken advantage of Napoleon's disturbances to declare independence. These hill people had neither sympathy nor common interest with the Mexicans in their next little oasis thousands of miles south of here. These people's only ties—and those long strained— were with Spain which lay still farther.

"It would solve your problems," Mrs. Lowery said.

"I beg your pardon?"

"To sell the ranch. You could take your share and be on your way. With our share Malcolm and I could find a less adventuresome life somewhere else."

"I thought you were determined not to sell."

She sighed. "What am I to do?"

The boy roused from his lethargy. "Fight!" he snarled. "Git them Double-O rannies before they hooraw us right out of the territory."

Rudge shrugged. "'Twould seem we have little choice. Can you shoot?"

"Ain't no great shakes with a pistol," the boy said. "But I can hit what I aim at with a rifle."

"He really is a crack shot," his sister contributed.

The old woman's stringy mutton and chile stew fulfilled Rudge's worst expectations. He wiped his forehead and wondered momentarily if this concoction was melting the wax out of his ears. The others ate without comment, devouring the luscious-appearing but totally wind-filled *sopapillas* with evident delight. He passed up a second helping and sipped scalding coffee until the fire departed from his mouth, then lit a cheroot. When Malcolm went to see to a champing mustang just outside the fortified camp area, he asked, "Is the boy truly dependable enough to protect you?"

"You are leaving?" Either Mrs. Lowery was a consummate actress or she really didn't care that deeply whether Rudge stayed or not. He looked to his Colts and checked his pockets for extra cartridges.

"Only temporarily," he said. "And should I attract any attention I'll try not to draw it in this direction."

"Are you sure that's wise, Mr. Rudge?"

"Is it wise to wait for a superior force to cut us off from our water? This hilltop is no more tenable than was your estate down below. Only here you stand less chance of being surprised."

"I suppose you're right, Mr. Rudge."

"If I don't come back within a reasonable time, I suggest you get back down to Soda Springs and see what can be salvaged with our two visitors." He remembered and handed her the letter.

As he rode off into gathering darkness Rudge didn't know whether he was right or not. Common sense told him there were easier ways of acquiring a third of $20,000—or whatever was being offered for the ruins of this ranch. He urged his mustang down the watercourse and, a couple of miles downstream, passed the cutoff where the trail from Soda Springs ran into this valley.

It would not be difficult, he saw, to scrape up enough dirt at this spot to send the water running off down toward the town—where it would disappear into the loose desert soil long miles before it could do anything to improve the potability of Soda Springs.

The stars and the lightning bugs came out in force, and the more he considered it, the more Rudge suspected water diversion would not be necessary. The people downstream would be back soon enough once the word spread that some Maclendons had returned.

And meanwhile, if he had a brain in his head, Rudge would keep right on riding, toward San Francisco—anywhere away from this viper's nest. Was he never to be free of violence—other men's troubles? There was nothing to hold him here. Nothing at all—except one third of $20,000. Not even that if Mrs. Lowery intended to hang on. How does one spend a sheep?

"But you helped create the problem." It was his recording angel again.

"Like hell I did! Lowery wrote that letter while I was still making my discreet way up through Texas—and whatever happened to that quiet idea? I've left a trail now that even a blindfolded Pinkerton could follow."

"But you killed Lowery."

"And did the poor woman a favor. Would she be better off if I'd let him kill me?"

His recording angel's reply was lost when his mustang stumbled and nearly went down in loose gravel. Man and horse struggled to maintain their relative positions for a moment. Rudge recaptured the stirrup he had lost and spent half a minute murmuring the quiet nonsense one uses to soothe horses and women.

When the mustang tired of buckjumping he urged it around to see what loose gravel was doing along this smooth, damp, earthed path that bordered the creek.

Now that was most extraordinary. He decided his recording angel had not been so engrossed in argument as not to have one eye still open for his well-being. He squinted in the starlight and saw how close the mustang had come to stepping into another open grave. The horse had lost its footing in gravel freshly shoveled from that hole.

Rudge forced the horse to stand quiet for a moment while he listened. There were tiny packrat noises amid the bushes but he could see nothing more threatening. Still, some instinct warned him that there was danger nearby. He squinted slightly to one side and watched which way the mustang's ears would swivel.

They did not move, save for the constant twitching from lightning bugs and other insects along the streambed. Rudge wanted to dismount and find out if there was anyone in this grave but something kept warning him to get out of here.

Getting old, he thought. Never used to fidget like this. He studied the velvety blackness, listening over the faint murmur of the creek for any hint that he and the horse were not alone. There was none. Still, something primordial riveted him to the mustang's placid back.

It was silly. Irrational. And as Rudge sat his horse and dithered in the darkness he knew that something profound was happening inside him. If he gave in to this crazy, upstairs-in-the-dark mood he could probably find reasons to justify whatever course he took. Nobody else would ever know. But Rudge would know. The knowledge would erode his self-confidence until soon everyone would know.

"*Don't!*" his recording angel warned.

Rudge ignored the warning. But there was little profit in being totally foolhardy. He had a sudden inspiration of how he might look into that hole with the least possible exposure to himself. He rummaged in his pocket and found a seven-day stink.

He struck the match on his boot sole and tossed it. There was a faint phosphorescent streak as the sizzling matchhead arced down into the open grave, looking for all the world like one more lightning bug. It struck bottom six feet down and lay sizzling and sputtering another half eternity. Finally the sulfur match burst into flame.

The hole was not empty. He caught a quick glimpse of old newspaper, assorted trash, an empty crate. Then the match caught the edge of a piece of newspaper and suddenly the light was too bright for Rudge's taut nerves. He neckreined the mustang away and spurred the startled beast into a gallop as he stretched out to lay over its neck.

A hundred yards away Rudge reined in, ashamed at the panic that had overcome him. If there had been anyone around here to see him, that flare of light was sufficient for him to see which way the mustang's ears were pointing. It was a damnfool thing he had done to gallop a horse through the darkness. What if he had stumbled into another hole?

The horse slowed and walked a dozen more paces before coming to a halt. Rudge looked back. The fire in the grave was sending a wavering skyward beam like some nascent volcano.

Lost your nerve, he told himself. You'd better hit the trail for San Francisco. What was it that had frightened him? He had never been the kind of man who spooked for no reason, like a young horse or a herd of longhorns.

Then as the grave exploded with a sound like a battery of cannon, sending a skyward fountain of fire he knew he had been at least partly right. A mitrailleusade of gravel and small stones peppered Rudge and the mustang and he knew he should have obeyed his instincts. He should have made tracks out of here. He should never have lit that lucifer.

XIII

The horse lost its last vestige of patience. First, it had been forced to stampede blindly through the darkness, and now this sudden blaze, this noise, this canister shot of gravel, this utter fool of a man in the saddle. The mustang shrieked and went skyward sunfishing once before it landed stiff-legged. Rudge wondered momentarily if his teeth were still in their sockets. Even more, he wondered where his stirrups had gone.

It was not the time for gallant, no-hands horsemanship. He clawed leather uninhibitedly and managed to stay aboard while the mustang demonstrated its repertory of ways to shed a saddle. A stirrup swung upward and banged Rudge in the hip. He would limp for a week even if this long-suffering animal did not throw him.

The mustang stopped bucking and charged through thick undergrowth along the creekbed. Rudge captured one stirrup and lay over the animal's neck, concentrating on overhanging limbs. The horse went between two trees—or had he split one tree in two? Rudge received another crushing blow on his stirrup-banged hip.

Finally horse and man were motionless, panting in the starlight. "Truly sorry about that," Rudge apologized. "You've every right to expect a man to be at least as intelligent as you are."

He spent considerably more time abasing himself before the heaving mustang accepted his lame excuses. And the excuses, Rudge realized, were not half as lame as he was going to be as soon as he began to feel all the outrages his body had received.

Couldn't anything go right? Fine figure of a man he was going to make now when he came crawling back to the Maclendon camp. He didn't know exactly what he had set out to accomplish but surely it was not to set off an explosion that could be heard for miles—not to come limping back with bruises that would disable him for a week and a horse that would probably come up as lame as he was.

Whoever had laid that trap was going to be around soon to see what he had caught. And even with undamaged Colts, Rudge was not himself undamaged. He studied the skyline and spurred the still-resentful mustang halfway up the hillside, hoping to find a way back to the Maclendons that would neither leave him open to attack on the creekside trail, nor exposed on the skyline. By the time he was within hailing distance of the camp he was beginning to hurt.

"Sounded like you blew them Oostenvelds sky-high," Malcolm enthused once they were finished with the tiresome business of advancing-to-be-recognized.

But when Rudge got his mustang hobbled and unsaddled and dragged his limping way in between the buckboards the boy's sister saw it more accurately. "Looks more like they blew you sky-high," she said. She spoke to the old woman—too rapidly for Rudge to follow. The old woman rummaged about in his traps and found the bottle of Green River.

"Thank God for women with sufficient perspicacity to put first things first," Rudge sighed as he upended the bottle. He pulled off his boots and Colts and wrapped up in his blanket where, having gauged his dosage to a nicety, he managed to sleep. When he looked up again the Big Dipper had rotated half the night.

How did they know I was coming? For someone to know that much about what went on inside his head was more than Rudge was capable of believing. Not even his recording angel could have known Rudge would ride after dark past that particular spot. Nor could anyone have known the blue devils would cause him to toss a match instead of just jump down in the hole and feel around—*a rattlesnake?*

Rudge had seen this sort of trap before—had helped devise them when the fortunes of war disposed that his positions would be overrun by a looting enemy. But to tailor a fool's petard to the exact position Rudge had taken at that moment . . . His hackles rose in sudden *frisson* as he pondered the possibility of something more than human. In the distance a coyote howled and the sound shamed Rudge back into sanity.

There were no supernatural forces; therefore nobody had set that charge just to blow him up. Instead, he had blundered into something not intended for him. Perhaps not for anyone else either. And now if they would just leave him alone long enough for the stirrup-shaped bruise on his hip to disappear, perhaps he could venture out and find out what or whom that bomb was intended for. Not just leave him alone—leave alone all the lame and halt who still adhered to the Maclendon cause.

"Mr. Rudge, are you awake?"

"Unfortunately," he admitted.

"Are you—are your injuries serious?"

"Nothing a few days' rest won't cure."

There was a silence, then the soft voice mused, "I wonder which of us will be up and about first."

"How are you feeling?"

"Better. I believe it was mostly the heat and the loss of blood. Since we've stopped traveling and are once more in the mountains I feel much recruited."

"And still resolved to hold fast?"

"With God's help."

"Yes," he said absently. "That's always helpful too."

"You are not a believer, Mr. Rudge?"

"That would depend on what you're asking me to believe in."

"Why the one God, of course!"

"Brahma, Vishnu, or Shiva?"

And that was the end of that conversation. He lay staring up at the stars, thinking about everything except what he ought to: how many days before the light of the moon again, if he would ever find some place where a man might feel like settling down. Perhaps he ought to try Australia. Was there any place farther away? He would look into it when he reached San Francisco.

Gradually Mrs. Lowery's breathing turned deep and regular like the others' and he had the night to himself again. He found himself wondering over the fortuitous appearance of those two bankers. Was twenty thousand a reasonable offer for this place? Under the circumstances, with the Maclendon holdings surrounded by usurping freebooters . . .

It was too reasonable. Maclendon's will had mentioned ten thousand head and get. With sheep worth a dollar a head and the ranch in working order the price might have been fair. With the ranch converted to ashes, herders and sheep scattered to the four winds. Those bankers were not members of a charitable order.

"Mr. Lowery consorted openly with my father's enemies."

What did Maclendon's enemies and his son-in-law know that the surviving Maclendons didn't seem to know? The old man had told Rudge he knew who killed him. It might have been more helpful if he had told Rudge why.

The bankers would have stopped in Soda Springs. Undoubtedly, they would have picked up local news in the process of getting directions and outfitting for the final stage of their long ride up from Santa Fe. They would have to have been singularly obtuse not to have heard about the problems the Maclendons were facing.

Rudge sighed. He just plain didn't know. His hip was aching. Every part of him was aching from the jolting that outraged mustang had given him. He was not going to sleep any more tonight. How much more could he hurt back on his feet? He slipped out of his blanket and saddled a fresh mustang who would not be inclined to remind him of his shortcomings earlier this evening.

"Again, Mr. Rudge?"

"Again," he growled, and forced his aching body into the saddle.

The first hundred yards downhill were such unadulterated agony that once the animal was plodding its careful way along the creekbed trail he scarcely noticed the pain. There was some danger in taking this path instead of picking his way among the rocks halfway up the hillside, but he assumed that if anyone had come to investigate the blast, by now they would have been up here poking around the Maclendon ashes looking for whomever . . .

He passed the Soda Springs cutoff, rode another couple of hip-throbbing miles, and caught the acrid whiff of burnt powder. He slowed the already barely moving mustang and they felt their way past the enlarged grave. Time passed until, with sunrise scarcely another hour away, the moon finally rose and the horse could trot.

The creek was no larger here than it had been up above. Slightly smaller, if anything. He remembered how enthusiastic Malcolm and Eusebio had been about diverting water away from the people downstream. The valley was still a half-mile wide but down here the grass was not so thoroughly sheeped off as it had been on the approach to the Maclendons'.

Hissing with pain, he dismounted and studied the grass. It had been grazed over but a hungry cow could still have gotten months of nourishment from the grass that Rudge's horse was eating. How much range did the penny-farthing brand claim? How many head were they running? There was not the slightest sign or smell of cow around here.

He rode another couple of miles and knew he could not be all that far from the penny-farthing headquarters. He sniffed but if there was any smoke the dead calm air was not wafting it his way. Behind him gray dawn began augmenting the moon and he saw that his earlier suspicions were verified: plenty of grass and not enough cow plop.

His body's accumulated grudges were abruptly demanding satisfaction. Unless this were to be just another wild-goose chase he had to hole up for the day. He glanced up the hillside. Then as the creek meandered around another gentle turn he saw his first cow.

It was a rangy, warble-infested longhorn. People up here had obviously not yet started to improve the breed with imported bulls. He halted his horse and studied the valley ahead. He was about to push on when abruptly a black smudge erupted just around the bend. He edged forward as the smoke lessened and began turning gray. Somebody had just lit the breakfast fire in a pole building up ahead.

Beyond the building another canyon branched into that valley. It was a place where he could hide among the trees. Then he knew he'd better not. Any place that attractive would draw cattle, who would draw riders, who would probably have dogs with them this close to the ranch. He studied the barren hillside and began urging his mustang up, following the slope to stay out of sight of the penny-farthing ranch. Somewhere below him a cock was crowing.

Twenty minutes later, feeling vaguely foolish, Rudge lay atop a bald hill a quarter mile above what he assumed was the penny-farthing spread. He had picketed his mustang on the other side of the hill, out of sight of the ranch buildings, leaving the beast to graze with the bit dangling to one side but bridle on and otherwise ready. He had loosened the cinch, which was as much as he dared risk for the horse's comfort.

Beside him Rudge had a single canteen. The sun was coming up brighter than limelight and he suspected—hoped —he was in for a long day. If anyone were to venture up here he would be in plain sight. But, providing he suppressed his desire for a cheroot, there was no reason for anyone to venture up here. Behind him the horse snorted.

Which made little difference. There were a dozen mounts in the pole corral below, all making their own morning noises as men straggled from the bunkhouse and walked past the corral toward the cookhouse.

It was the sorriest excuse for a ranch that Rudge had looked on for some time. The "big" house was a cabin that could not be more than a single room and loft, unless some-one had made interior alterations that did not show joinings in the log walls. The boars' nest could not hold more than a dozen men unless they were sleeping double. One corner of the cookhouse roof sagged where a log had come out of its notch and was propped in permanent dislocation lest the whole building collapse.

The corral poles were chewed nearly through in spots and there were no spares piled anywhere in view. The watering trough was equally abraded until it held half what it ought to. There was a rusting mower behind the corral but no slightest hint of haystack. Which meant somebody had used the last of it before the new grass had come in.

In stark contrast to all this was the staked and trenched outline of a more ambitious "big" house a few feet behind the cabin. Smithy, storage sheds, everything that related to the stock or hired hands was in the final stages of dissolu-tion. And on this base someone was planning a mansion. The stakes behind the "big" house were fresh split, the string taut between them, the sides of the shallow trench straight and new-spaded. Rudge reached for a cheroot, then remembered it was broad daylight now.

Men straggled from the cookhouse belching and picking their teeth. They went to the corral to rope and saddle their mounts and shake early morning kinks out of them.

A horse snorted in Rudge's ear. He rolled over, wondering how his mount had manged to pull its picket. But the horse was not his. A mouse mustang with full saddle marks was looking down at him. The horse was hobbled.

All Rudge needed was for one of those men to come blundering up here after a horse. He scooted back out of sight and the horse followed. "No, blast it, go home!" he hissed, and slapped the mouse on the rump. The mustang spun and snatched his hat off.

Of all the times to run into somebody's pet with a favorite trick! The mouse-colored animal still wanted to play. It came close. Rudge reached for his hat. The mustang tossed his head and hobble-jumped out of reach and Rudge discovered that "he" was a mare.

Rudge burst into sweat as his bruised hip began demanding back pay. He struggled to catch the mare but the way he was limping even a hobbled horse was too much. The mouse was heading downhill in hobbled jumps like a slow-motion gallop. The horse was heading straight for the men and the corral. Rudge's *sevillano* hat was still gripped firmly between huge grinning teeth.

XIV

Rudge consigned whoever taught the mustang that trick to the low-rent district of hell. In another second the beast would have his *sevillano* clear down to the corral. It was the only hat of its kind in these parts. If the men down below hadn't seen it in Soda Springs, chances were at least one or two of them had seen it the last time he had shot his way out of a penny-farthing confrontation.

He whistled, praying the men down below would be too busy roping and saddling their fullcock morning mounts to note one more noise. When the mouse mustang halted and turned to hobble-hop back uphill, he made a mental vow not to argue the next time with his recording angel.

The horse topped the rise and came to where Rudge stood just out of sight of the spread below. This time the horse dropped the hat at his feet. Rudge picked it up. He almost put it on, then knew he'd better not press his luck.

And now the damned beast wouldn't go away. If it was one of those men's favorites, surely somebody had seen it halfway down the hill. Sure as hell somebody was going to be up here in another minute. He ought to tighten cinch and make tracks on his own horse. But he couldn't face the thought of limping back once more empty-handed to the Maclendon camp.

"Go away, you silly beast!" he hissed. The accursed animal was nuzzling him, trying to get into his pocket. "I haven't any sugar, damn it! Here, have a cheroot." Maybe the taste of one of those vile black *compostelas* would encourage the horse to transfer its affections.

The horse liked cheroots. It was nuzzling him for another one. He slapped the mouse mare with his hat. It backed off a dozen feet to stare accusingly. He charged it, flapping his hat, and the pain made him gasp. He sank to his knees and for a moment there were two suns. But at least it worked. The mouse-colored mare had finally had enough of him. She was hopping off over the ridge and back down toward the ranch.

Then as his eyes cleared he knew it was too late. Somebody was galloping uphill. Somebody was yelling, "Nellie, goldang it, where you off to now?" A panting bay and rider burst over the hill, nearly on top of him. Rudge was still on his knees, struggling to focus his vision. The sun was getting to him. He put on his hat.

He sensed that the man on horseback was more startled than he was. Without conscious thought Rudge had Colts in hands, aiming at the man and horse that kept slipping out of focus.

"Oh Jesus," the man on horseback gasped, "the Limey!"

Rudge did not move. Still on his knees, a Colt in each hand, he waited for the pain to go away. Finally his eyes were clear again. This bay gelding was totally uninterested in men's affairs. It turned to nibble at the mouse mare's tail. The man astride the bay was only a boy. He seemed paralyzed, hands not raised but crossed over his chest as if he thought he could intercept lead that way. "Been waiting for you," Rudge said. "Come on down and tell me all the news."

The boy stared. His Adam's apple bobbed but he could not speak. Rudge gestured with one Colt. The boy managed to dismount. "Sit down and make yourself comfortable," Rudge said. "Select a pose you'll be happy with throughout eternity."

"Y-you ain't gonna kill me?"

"Can you give me one reason why I should not?"

"I didn't know it was her horse."

"Oh? Who's *her?*"

"Uh, I don't know."

Very slowly, Rudge began squeezing the trigger of one pistol.

"Miz Lowery!"

"Well fancy that!" Rudge let off the cock and holstered the pistol. The other remained pointing at the boy. "Too bad," he sighed.

"What's too bad?"

"Surely you know what happens to horse thieves."

From his totally craven air the boy obviously knew. He was about seventeen—about Malcolm Maclendon's age—with a broad freckled face that just missed being handsome. "Do you have a name?" Rudge asked. When the boy did not reply he added, "Always feel down in the mouth when I see a headboard marked 'Unknown.'"

"But they was all doin' it," the boy protested.

"Then they shall all most assuredly end their days kicking at the end of a rope." Rudge glanced around, then returned to his theme. "The fortunate are those who have a horse whipped from beneath them. Usually their sufferings are terminated within a quarter of an hour. But others whom a merciful God singles out for especial favor in the next life are slowly hoisted by the neck. Considering the augmented glory that awaits them, it's most extraordinary how they cling—often as long as an hour—to this miserable existence."

"I didn't know it was her horse!"

"But surely you knew it was not yours." The mouse-colored mare in question tried to snatch Rudge's hat again. "Changing the subject for a moment," he continued, "have you ever seen a pair of pistols like these before?"

"Wush I'd never see'd 'em," the boy blubbered.

"Is that all the appreciation you can demonstrate for this crowning achievement of the gunsmith's art?"

"What difference does it make? If'n you don't hang me you'll shoot me."

"Ah, but that is precisely the difference," Rudge explained. "No doubt you're familiar with the original .44-caliber Navy Colt. Now these have been bored out another hundredth of an inch. The percussion-cap cylinder has been exchanged for a bored-through cylinder to hold quick-loading cartridges. And the ramrod is now replaced with an ejector. Often I find myself reloading for the third time while the possessors of cap and ball pistols are still deploring the misfire that cost them their drab and wretched lives."

Rudge drew breath and, from this tiny platform of truth, soared into realms of pure fantasy. "The Theurs Conversion is well known in London. Less well known is the composition of these prodigious cartridges. You may have heard one last night when I was forced to dispute the right of way with some blackguard."

The boy lost another shade of color and Rudge knew the sound of that explosion had carried at least this far. "Uh, was it Wes?" he managed.

"I couldn't say. Is Wes a few bits of bone and blood?" He paused, then added, "I did find the somewhat worn-down heel of one boot."

The boy's teeth were chattering. "You gonna blow me up like that?"

"That depends on how quickly you can pull my horse's stake and tighten his cinch. Should you attempt to hide on the opposite side of the beast I shall regretfully sacrifice the animal since you've brought me yours."

"You'd shoot your own horse?"

"Only if you force me to. The thickness of a horse tends to mitigate the force of even a Theurs explosive bullet. Instead of an instantaneous death you might suffer nearly as long as will all those misguided men below once the day of reckoning arrives. I recommend that you stay on this side of the horse."

To Rudge's no great surprise the boy did exactly as told. While he was busy cinching the mustang's saddle and putting the bit back in Rudge drew a deep breath and forced himself to stand. By the time the boy returned with the mustang he could see clearly again. He had no intention of trying to mount while this boy watched. "Get that mare now," he instructed. "Take off her hobbles and rig a lead rope."

"You gonna take her back to the Maclendons?"

"You are."

Though not delighted with the prospect, clearly the boy found it preferable to dying. He did as told, then once more faced Rudge who stood holding the reins of his mount in one hand and a Colt in the other.

"Opie!" somebody shouted from downhill. "Opie, God-damn it, where'd you git off to this time?"

The boy stared blankfaced at Rudge.

"If necessary, of course I'll kill you," Rudge said conversationally. "It all depends on how quickly and quietly you can head back upstream without anyone seeing you. By the way, a Theurs Conversion cartridge explodes at point of impact so distance makes no difference. But should you get more than a mile ahead of me it might be construed as prima facie evidence of evil intent."

"I won't," the boy hastened. He mounted his horse and began leading the hat-stealing mare back toward the Maclendons'. Rudge waited till the boy's back was turned before mounting his own mustang. He gritted his teeth and waited for the first fine agony to leave his hip.

"Opie, Goddamn it, you get back down here!"

"I'm coming," Rudge called, and spurred his mustang after the boy.

He had been afraid one of the penny-farthing riders would be herding cattle up this way but they had all apparently gone up into the other canyon. He caught up with the boy and hung on his trail a hundred feet behind. The mouse-colored mare was tossing her head and making a spoiled nuisance of herself, at times nearly jerking the boy from the saddle.

"*You didn't have to lay it on all that thick.*" It was his recording angel again.

Rudge remembered his vow not to argue.

"*Scaring the poor lad right out of his wits. And whence all that randygazoo about exploding bullets? You know perfectly well the Theurs Conversion is only from cap and ball to cartridge. Really now!*"

"Really yourself! Would you rather I leave enough spunk in him for the lad to make a run for it?"

"*But really! The poor misguided lad deserves a decent chance at life.*"

"So do the Maclendons. And if that poor misguided lad takes it in his mind to light a shuck, do you really expect me to let him go?"

"*But charity—*"

"Begins at home. And where were you when that accursed mustang was using my hip for a splitting wedge? If you've nothing to do but devil me, why don't you get back up there and see that poor woman recruited from her wound?"

There was no reply. Rudge endured the throbbing ache in his hip and wondered what he was going to do with the boy. Much as the young ruffian might deserve hanging, Rudge did not want to be responsible for yet another stripling's death.

Up ahead the boy reached the grave that had blown up in Rudge's face. He gave it an incurious glance and continued. Rudge spurred closer, wondering how he could initiate a casual conversation without dulling the bright edge of terror he had so carefully instilled in this born-to-be-hung boy. "Did you dig it?" he asked.

From the boy's unfeigned surprise Rudge knew he had not. "Do you know who did?" Once more the boy did not really have to reply. "And apart from stealing Maclendon horses, what other deviltry have you been up to?"

"Nothin'." Terror had been converted into a sullen resignation.

"Killing sheep?"

No reply.

"Killing herders?"

"Ain't nothin' wrong with killin' sheepmen," the boy muttered.

"Nothing at all," Rudge agreed, "save that to shoot one without provocation will get you hanged just as promptly as horse thievery."

"Don't give a care," the boy grumped. "You're gonna kill me anyhow. You and them goldang high and mighty Maclendons!"

"High and mighty?"

No reply.

"Of what nature was the affront?"

The boy didn't understand him. Rudge rephrased the question: "What'd the Maclendons ever do to you?"

"Goddamn Yankees!"

Rudge began to understand. But how provincial could these people be? "Am I a Yankee too?" he asked.

"Dunno what you are. But I bet you never lost no war."

It required some effort for Rudge not to explode in cracked laughter. "Not one," he admitted, and did not bother to explain that he had lost two and seemed well on his way to losing a third. "You suffered loss and personal injury during the late conflict?" he asked. The boy could not have been over seven when that conflict ended. What was Rudge going to do with him?

"Lost me som'p'n all right."

His childhood, no doubt. Rudge remembered the year after the war, when broken families in a desolated country had eaten juney bugs while waiting for a crop. Rudge had lost something too. "I wonder if there is any possible way your life can be saved?" he mused.

The boy did not appear to have heard him.

"At home they still hang boys for stealing sheep."

Still no reply.

"And then there are the workhouses for minor offenses—such as being born poor. Don't fancy you'd know the meaning of skilly?"

"I s'pose it's somethin' they whup you with."

"Internally," Rudge explained. "Perhaps you'd know it as mush. It's all you'll be getting. They keep you from asking for more by taking care that it's always burnt. The lads can't eat it at first. Takes a few twelve-hour days on a treadmill to perk up their appetites."

The boy's eyes remained fixed on his saddle horn. "Can't be too bad," he finally muttered. "Leastways they give it to you once a day, don't they?"

Rudge had been beaten at his own game. He was thankful that the boy was riding ahead where he could not see the sudden moisture that filled Rudge's eyes. Perhaps his recording angel was right. This wretched creature ought to be given some kind of a chance at life.

XV

The three horses plodded along the creekside trail with Rudge in the rear. He struggled to remember what his mind had been like at that age. But Rudge had known schooling and the advantages of wealth. He wondered if life was any easier for those who had known only poverty. At least they had never faced an abrupt plunge into misery. But mostly, he wondered what he was going to do with this sullen boy.

"You've killed a multitude of others even younger," his recording angel taunted.

"All of whom were actively engaged in returning the compliment," Rudge muttered.

"Huh?"

"Nothing. I was talking to somebody else."

"Ain't nobody else."

Rudge was suddenly inspired. If people with impressive strings of letters behind their names would buy shares in gold mines, in railroads, in coal-oil wells they had never seen, surely Rudge could keep from making a fool of himself before this child of nature who needed help to write his name. "I was addressing my Portable Intelligencer," he explained.

"Your what?"

"You've heard of the telegraph, haven't you?"

The boy 'lowed as how he had.

"This is a new kind. It works without wires or any clickety-clack. You have only to talk into it."

"Yeah? Who you talkin' to?"

"The sheriff down in Soda Springs."

The boy wavered on the edge of disbelief.

"Yes?" Rudge addressed himself to his mount's twitching ears. "Yes. I see. You'll be waiting?"

"How come I can only hear you?" the boy demanded.

"You're not spliced into the machine," Rudge explained. "Yes, sheriff. I'll give him—hmmm. What can I give him?

"No. Sorry. Not a scrap of paper about me. Perhaps if I describe him—?"

Rudge waited a decent interval while the boy turned in his saddle to stare. He was still unsure whether to swallow one more miracle in an era that was bursting with innovations. But the boy had heard older men speak matter-of-factly of telegraphs, of gas lights, steamboats, and trains. The boy was living in an age when anything was possible.

"He's about seventeen." Rudge continued addressing his mount's ears. "Ugly little wart. Straw hat and no soles to his straight boots. He'll be riding a dun mare about half as old as his saddle." Rudge waited a moment, then made a spinning gesture as if he were shutting off some invisible steam valve. He turned to address the boy. "The sheriff promises me that he will not shoot you as you ride into town," he explained.

"Who says I'm goin'?"

"I'd take you in myself, just to make sure they give you a quick and merciful hanging," Rudge said, "except that I'll be busy here making sure none of the other culprits get away."

"Other what?"

"Your friends back there at the ranch."

"What you gonna do to them?"

"They're grown men," Rudge explained. "Old enough to know what they're doing. Now you—"

"They gonna hang me down there?"

"Of course they will. But your friends back at the ranch won't get off so easily. Now remember, if you try to sneak around town the sheriff's sure to follow. When he catches up the posse's going to be out of sorts from having to get out of their nice cool chairs to ride across the desert after a half-grown horse thief." Rudge paused for emphasis. "You're lucky to be getting out of this valley right now. So, whatever you do, don't try to sneak past Soda Springs and get down into Texas where all the bad men go for a fresh start where nobody knows them."

Rudge paused and managed not to smile as he watched these bits of information enter the boy's head and congeal into a usable pattern. He wondered if his own face had been that readable when he was seventeen. "Well fancy that," he added. "We've reached the cutoff already."

"You just gonna send me into town alone?" The boy was incredulous.

"That's right. You're a smart enough lad not to even think of coming back up into this country and being carved into little pieces with a redhot knife along with all those other blackguards. Just present yourself to Sheriff Jason and he'll see that you're properly hanged. And I don't want you even thinking about that next waterhole eighteen miles on the other side of Soda Springs."

The boy assured Rudge that no such thought would ever cross his mind. Rudge sat his horse at the cutoff watching for half an hour until boy and horse disappeared in the shimmering distance.

"Ought to be ashamed of yourself!" his angel said.

"Perhaps," Rudge replied. "I'm sure it would have been safer to shoot him."

His recording angel did not reply.

Rudge tugged on the hat-stealing mare's lead rope and began the final stretch back to camp. His hip was throbbing and for brief moments his mount seemed to have two heads and four ears superimposed on each other like a bad engraving.

He studied the sun. Midmorning already. Shouldn't be exposed out here by daylight. What if one of those penny-farthing riders were to come looking for the boy? Shouldn't have wasted half an hour there at the cutoff making sure a frightened-unto-piddling boy would not come back. If Rudge was reading him aright, that boy would not stop moving until he was deep into Texas, where he might possibly live long enough to become an exemplary citizen and hang horse thieves.

When Rudge reached the Maclendon ashes there were no tiresome challenges or countersigns. He urged the horses uphill to the camp between upended buckboards and discovered that Malcolm was gone. Mrs. Lowery was on her feet again, looking much recovered.

"Blossom!" she shrieked, and threw her arms about the hat-stealing mouse-mustang. Rudge unsaddled and hobbled his mount. He found a spot behind one buckboard where the sun would not penetrate for a few hours and lay down. He drew his *sevillano* over his face.

When he awoke Malcolm was still gone.

"Told him to stay here and watch over you and the old woman," Rudge growled.

Mrs. Lowery squinted past the late afternoon sun. She turned and squatted beside Rudge. "It's my fault," she said. "He was getting restless with nothing to do and I'm feeling much recruited so—"

"Where is he?"

"He was going upstream to make sure the other horses didn't stray too far."

"Upstream?"

She nodded again. Rudge noted that even after exhaustion, illness, and bereavement the red-haired Anges Lowery was a woman of parts—none of which seemed to be missing.

"Is there any way someone could get up past here from downstream without being seen?"

"It's possible. Not likely though."

Rudge looked at her.

"I've ridden these hills since I was fourteen," she explained. "Mostly on Blossom. You were so worn out I didn't want to delay your sleep with tiresome effusions. But I do thank you, Mr. Rudge. Did you have to kill anyone to get her back?"

"Not exactly." He explained what had happened.

"And you're sure the boy will not return?"

Rudge shrugged.

"Somehow I had expected different of you."

"Do you think I enjoy devouring raw children?"

"I'm happy to learn that you do not."

"Have you achieved any sort of tally of the Maclendon holdings?"

"Only some inspired guessing," she said. "Rosaura says those few herders who remained when I went into town have mostly given up and left the country."

So that was the old woman's name. "And the sheep?"

"The herders went because there was nothing left for them to do."

"So the penny-farthings have been killing sheep too?"

"I beg your pardon, Mr. Rudge?"

"Those scoundrels downstream. Oostenveld, I believe."

"Yes, I'm sure they're the ringleaders. There are other smaller holdings. Probably none of them is above eating Maclendon mutton instead of their own beef from time to time but we've never caught them at anything worse. But why do you call them penny— What was the word?"

Rudge explained about the bicycle with a large front wheel and a tiny one behind, proportioned like the huge English penny and the smaller farthing.

"I'd never thought of it that way," she mused. "It does look like one."

"Have you ever wondered why they're so determined to force you out of this country?"

Mrs. Lowery seemed taken aback by the question. "I suppose it's sheep against cattle," she said.

"Can you think of no other reason?"

"No, Mr. Rudge."

He left it at that. With Malcolm not there to run errands, their hilltop "fort" was low on water. He loaded a horse with every conceivable container and, after a careful look around, went down to the creek.

Had the penny-farthing scoundrels learned already that another of their riders was missing? How many of theirs had died in the last few days? He would have to ask Mrs. Lowery how many of the victims of that Golden Eagle shooting scrape had been ◯o men. Either of the pair he had packed back into town? What of the next lot who had openly flaunted their brand? He knew he had killed one and damaged another. Could they possibly believe the battle was over, that the surviving Maclendons would give up and depart after one look at the ashes?

Fat chance! They would know that he, the Limey, was still alive. Everyone in the country, including some freighter, knew Rudge was alive. Soon they would know that he had been reduced to bushwhacking. Again.

"You might have paid attention to business."

"You again?" In spite of having slept several hours Rudge's hip was still sore and he was in no mood for discussions with his recording angel.

"Instead of spending all your time scaring that poor lad out of a year's growth you might have asked him how many there were at the penny-farthing—how many wounded, how many head of cattle?"

Rudge sighed and continued filling canteens and water bags. If he hadn't been so tired perhaps he could have interrogated his captive in proper fashion. But it was too late now. He wondered if young Malcolm could have taken it into his head to circle around the camp and head downstream into mischief.

Suddenly it was cold. He looked up at a solid wall of cloud sweeping up from the south. By the time he finished filling canteens and got back uphill it was raining.

He sat huddled under a tarp with Mrs. Lowery and the old woman sourly watching clear, clean water pour from one sagging edge of their shelter. Less inclined to criticize the elements, old Rosaura scooted a cauldron underneath to catch it.

"Cheer up, Mr. Rudge."

"Is it that obvious?" He wondered if it had been this coming storm that made his hip ache so. Probably not. That only happened with old wounds like the one in his shoulder. "Will it last long?" he asked.

"They seldom do this time of year," Mrs. Lowery said.

But when late afternoon came, it was still raining and the boy was still gone. Rudge surveyed the horses who stood heads down, tied to upended buckboard wheels. It was time to let them graze and bring up fresh horses from the hobbled *remuda* that Malcolm was supposed to be looking after. "Keep your eyes open," he said, and mounted one. He wondered if Mrs. Lowery's wound had plagued her as much on the long ride up here as his hip was bothering him now. And where had those confounded horses gotten off to?

He didn't really expect an attack during a storm. Rain in this country must be too rare for anyone to get into the habit of working through it. But if he didn't round up those horses soon, he was going to end up in a darkness twice as black as last night when he had nearly stumbled into a pitful of explosives.

Finally, a couple of miles upstream, he found four horses standing heads down. He switched their hobbles to those he had brought from uphill and began riding and leading the new string back.

"What am I doing here?" he growled. "I can't spend a sheep in San Francisco."

Mrs. Lowery was a handsome woman. Promised to be more so once she recovered from the loss of her father, her husband, and some flesh in one armpit.

He thought forebodingly about Malcolm. That oddly si-

lent boy . . . abruptly Rudge knew why he was so quiet.
The boy had not planned to assassinate him. Malcolm had
been so drowned in disgust with this country and its problems that he wanted to join Rudge sight unseen—anything
to get away. Now his conscience was reminding him of the
fix in which he had been prepared to abandon his sister,
with neither husband nor father.

What fool's errand was the boy off on now? If he were to
blunder among the penny-farthing riders, Rudge had no il-
lusion that they would treat Malcolm with the consideration
that Rudge had shown one of theirs. Perhaps he ought to
have shot that half-grown horse thief after all. Sooner or
later he was going to have to extract retribution. They had
killed Maclendon sheep and shepherds. They had killed
Maclendon. Such people do not respond to sweet reason.

Probably they did not even respond to simple retaliation.
He had killed some of theirs. Still they kept on killing for
land they didn't especially need—not with those few head of
runty cattle. But if they did not fear the known, perhaps he
could induce them to fear the unknown.

He grinned at the abrupt realization that he already had a
good beginning at this game. Were they even now wondering how a boy and a horse could disappear within shouting
distance of the ranch house? When the weather improved,
he would go back downstream and see what else he could
do to assure them that Maclendons could rise from the
ashes. He was urging the new string of horses back toward
the "fort" when he heard a single shot.

XVI

Rudge halted the horses. With an unthinking reflex, he checked his Colts. He remembered the huge single-shot rifle and wondered if the redheaded woman would have knocked herself into the middle of next week firing it—torn herself open again.

Perhaps she had only intended the shot as a warning for Rudge. Would she have known enough to put the butt on the ground? He waited for a second shot and even as he waited he knew it might never come. She might be unconscious, bleeding, dying.

There was the sudden pop of a smaller caliber weapon and he knew it was no false alarm. He had thought nothing was going to happen until the rain was over. Should have known better. Hadn't he soldiered enough to know the first inviolable rule of warfare: that any important action must always be fought hip deep in mud during the century's worst weather?

Was it fighting that brought rain or did the chicken come after the egg? Was he going to sit here in the rain and ponder philosophy or was he going to do something to help the women? If he were up there with them, there was a fair chance they could fight off any attack. But the old woman probably didn't know how to shoot and couldn't see a target if she did. Mrs. Lowery . . . how many rounds could she put into the attackers before she collapsed?

And he had left them without horses! There was no way the women could escape that hilltop fort even if they were not yet surrounded. If he were to come clattering through the rain with three mustangs in tow it would require no great tracking skill for the penny-farthings to find him. Then he realized they would probably think he was up there with the women. There had to be some deviltry he could get up to down here behind the attackers. He slipped from the saddle and tied the horses to a bush, wincing as his game hip gave him another reminder.

The steady downpour suddenly became a cloudburst. He slogged through water and gathering darkness, reminding himself that if he could not see them, they would have just as much trouble seeing him. He made out the dim outlines of trees, the loom of the hillside, but unless he was extremely careful Rudge knew he could easily blunder face to face into one of the penny-farthings.

He stood still and listened. Nothing but the cow-on-a-flat-rock sound of rain. Rain by the bucketful—by the acre foot! How high would the creek be? At least he hadn't wasted effort trying to dam and divert it. He grinned wryly into the darkness. He had done one thing right.

Were the attackers drowned out? He had only heard that single bellow from a Springfield and the answering pop of a smaller weapon. Probably the attackers were as blinded as he was and were sitting tight waiting for this *aguacero* to end. Just beyond the edge of his perception he was hearing something. But with all the racket this shower was making it had to be his imagination.

Cold. Soaked through completely, he was starting to shiver. All he needed now was for his old malaria to start up again. He took a single step, feeling blindly, hoping for some slight shelter. Suddenly, even soaked through as he was, he felt a tingling all over his body—as if every hair was standing on end.

Barely in time he threw himself flat in the mud. The meadow was abruptly illuminated and his eardrums bursting from the sudden end-of-the-world sound of lightning point blank.

And I left the women camped on a hilltop!

He lay paralyzed in the mud, not even able to breathe. A moment passed and he could feel water trickle around his mouth and nose. So this was how one died of lightning—fully conscious but unable to move. Would he still be aware when they tossed him in a hole and started shoveling dirt in his face?

He would not. Already he could feel awareness starting to waver. He needed to breathe. His body was struggling to move. Then he felt his chest swell, a convulsive gasp and he was drowning from the water he had inhaled.

Coughing and retching, he managed to roll on his side where there was less chance of drowning. He wondered if he was deaf or if it had really stopped raining. Then as he coughed and vomited again awareness departed completely.

When Rudge awakened he was still unable to move. It was dark but now he could see stars in a clear sky and the wind had stopped. It was only when he tried to move that he understood what was wrong. He was not paralyzed. He was bound hand and foot.

But he was breathing. Must have been for some time, he guessed. He could still taste acrid vomit. Somebody had built a small pitch-pine fire more for light than heat. Somebody sat across the fire from him. He could not see the face. All Rudge could see was the worn-through soles of ill-fitting straight boots. The boots had switched feet so many times that only a tiny central nubbin remained of what had once been a high heel.

The last time he had seen boots like that was on the young horse thief he'd pointed toward Texas.

"Let's hear you talk to the sheriff on that porch of the hotel lyncher now," the boy said.

Rudge wondered if the lightning had affected his hearing. Then he remembered that he was the inventor of the portable intelligencer. Right now he could use one.

"Now what I want you to do," the boy said, "is git that fancypants down here."

"Surely you can't be referring to Mrs. Lowery—"

"You know goldang well who I mean. Stuckup fancypants with his new saddle and his crooked boots!"

"Yes," Rudge sighed. "I'm afraid I do. Now what did Malcolm ever do to you?"

"He keeps breathin' my air."

Rudge supposed it was inevitable. They were about the same age—probably the only boys of that age in the entire country. Natural companions and playmates. In the pig's eye! Rudge remembered how puzzled, hurt he had been when he had tried to renew ties with the ragged boys who had been his companions before he went off to school.

He had been ready to honor those ragged sons of the soil with his attention—the freewill offering of a young Rudge with splendid prospects and more important things to do than hunt up stick-in-the-mud boys who had yet to journey beyond their family farms. What right did those clods have to spurn him—turn their backs on a born Rudge? But they had. Whole lot of them had been mean and spiteful as Yankees. It had been the day that Rudge had started growing up.

The business of growing up was not yet completed, he guessed. He had let sentiment interfere with what he had instinctively known he had to do. He had not killed a horse thief so now the horse thief was going to kill him. And probably not quickly. "Don't know how I'll ever make it right with Mrs. Lowery," he muttered.

"Not that way. I want to hear you yell."

"I beg your pardon?"

"You tell that fancypants Malcolm to git hisself down here."

Rudge squinted and tried to clear the blurryness from his eyes. So the penny-farthings hadn't gotten Malcolm—so far at least. They thought he was up there with the women. So where on earth had Malcolm gotten himself off to?

The boy in the wornout boots got to his feet and walked around the tiny pine-knot fire. He kicked Rudge. Rudge wondered how this nascent dastard could have known which hip was already damaged. Then he remembered he only had two. Not the best of odds. "Hurry up!" the boy snarled and kicked him again.

First a stirrup, then a tree-splitting horse, now this boy's worn-out straight boot. Rudge wondered if he would ever walk again. If he didn't get his head to working and calm this spiteful young demon down, he would never get the chance to find out. "What exactly is it you expect me to do?" he asked.

"Tell Fancypants to git hisself down here."

Rudge shrugged as much as his bonds would let him. The movement brought a surge of burning tingle to his limbs. "Be happy to try," he said. "But can you think of one reason why he would consider paying any attention?"

"'Cause I'm gonna kill you. Tha's why!"

"And what is that to Malcolm?" When the boy paused in mid-kick Rudge continued, "You may not care much for the Maclendons, but try putting yourself in Malcolm's boots."

"Crooked boots?" the boy snarled.

Any other day of his life Rudge would have laughed. "Times change," he explained. "In ten years you'll not be able to buy those old-fashioned straight shoes. Pity in a way, since you can't change crooked shoes from one foot to the other and even out the wear. But if you live long enough, yes, even you and your friends will all end up wearing crooked shoes." The boy was cocking one of his worn straight boots to kick again.

"But what I was getting at," Rudge hastened, "is that I can lie here and call young Malcolm until the cows come home. I'm afraid nothing I might say can induce him to leave the safety of a fort where he can stand off the lot of you."

"Not even if I kill you?" The boy decided against kicking and cocked one of Rudge's pistols.

"Killing's easy," Rudge bluffed. "Obviously I'd've been better off if I'd not saved your life."

"I ain't gonna save yours."

"No reason why you should. Once the sheriff catches you you're going to hang anyway. Of course, horse thieves hang quick. They usually whip a horse from under them and the drop breaks a man's neck."

"I heard that flapdoodle already."

"On the other hand," Rudge continued, "for murder the law's liable to take a different view of hanging. Sometimes they just stand a man on his feet and start hauling him up off the ground. I hear they've a fellow down in Soda Springs who's so skillful at easing that rope along that the last murderer stood on tiptoes for nearly two hours before—" Rudge managed a laugh. "And then sometimes you'll get the real cute ones. They'll take half a day stringing you up and letting you down again. They do it twice for each man you've killed."

But the boy was not as impressionable as the last time Rudge had tried these tactics. Perhaps, Rudge decided, the arguments were more convincing when accompanied by a gun. The boy was building up a head of steam that would undoubtedly end in another kicking match.

"Tell Fancypants to git down here." It was the sullen growl of a loser who had yet to extract obedience from anyone.

"Certainly," Rudge said. "Just tell me what words to say. Shall I ask him to come down here and trade his life for that of the man who killed his brother-in-law?"

He had finally dropped a piece of information that stopped the boy for a moment. "You kilt who?"

"I believe his name was Lowery. He was husband to the

young lady who sits up there amid ample supplies of food, water, and ammunition."

"You're funnin' me."

"Why should I?"

There was a long silence while the boy fondled the Colt.

"They're hairtrigger, you know. If you insist on playing with them, why don't you look down the muzzle to see what happens when you breathe on it."

The boy put the cocked Colt on the ground with the muzzle pointed at Rudge.

"And don't forget that Theurs Conversion."

"That what?"

"Don't forget the explosive bullets. They're really not very good for closeup work. If you were to hit me at this distance the blast would undoubtedly destroy you too."

"I can back off."

"Of course you can. Why do you think I warn you?"

"I dunno. Why do you?"

"I'm still trying to save your wretched life."

"'Tain't me's gittin' fixed to die."

"Oh well—if you're going to be that way about it."

"Git on your feet."

"I'm afraid you'll have to at least partially untie me first."

The boy's frustration was so intense that for a moment Rudge thought he was going to be shot on the spot. He tried to keep a look of sweet reason on his face while the boy wrestled with his private demons and finally came cautiously around the fire. With a single slash he freed Rudge's legs.

Rudge rolled over and worked his legs, restraining the impulse to scream as blood began circulating. Finally he stood, bobbing and weaving like a drunken boxer, his arms still bound behind him. "Where to?" he asked thickly.

"Over where that Lowery bitch can see you."

Under the boy's prodding he stumbled a hundred yards

closer to the bottom of the hill. "Now jus' stand there a minute," the boy said.

While Rudge stood the boy piled fresh pitch sticks around
the guttering torch he carried. He was smarter than Rudge
had expected, for the boy piled the fire in front of Rudge and
before it could blaze up he had slipped behind Rudge into
the darkness. "Miz Lowery!" he yelled. "I got your fancy
man here. If'n you want him back whole, then you and your
brother better git on down here."

"No!"

It was a loud voice and it did not come from the hilltop.

Rudge turned. His eyes were blind from having faced the
pine-knot fire. But apparently his horse-stealing captor was
as surprised as Rudge. He half turned, peering into the
darkness. "Who is it?" he demanded.

He was pointing Rudge's Colt uncertainly at the darkness
behind them when there came a tiny piddling pop out of
that darkness. The Colt fell from the boy's hand and went
off with a noise that drowned out the original explosion. The
boy bent over.

XVII

Even as he stepped forward to kick his guns out of the boy's reach, Rudge had time to wonder how Mrs. Lowery had managed to sneak down from the hilltop without being caught by— Then abruptly he realized what was strange about the whole affair: this was not a full-scale raid by the penny-farthings. It was just the horse-thieving boy on his own.

Somewhere along the trail to Soda Springs the boy had recovered his courage, had come to see Rudge's cock-and-bull stories about portable intelligencers and exploding bullets for what they were. And if hell hath no fury like a woman scorned, then Satan has been remiss in analyzing the emotions of a maturing male who has just discovered somebody has made a fool of him.

Still the boy bent over, hands clutching his midsection. He was struggling to breathe, each labored breath a strange whistling little sob.

"I'm truly sorry you had to do it, Mrs. Lowery," Rudge managed. "Had I foreseen the consequences of an act of mercy—" But even as he wondered how the redhead had been able to pull the load from a heavy rifle and squib it off with such a faint explosion, he learned that he was mistaken.

It was Malcolm Maclendon who stepped from the darkness, a tiny, still-smoking saloon pistol in his hand. Stiff-legged, he strode to stand over the bent-over boy. The horse thief looked up and boy studied boy for a silent moment. "Hello, Opie," Malcolm said. "Does it hurt?"

The horse thief nodded, unable to speak.

"Good," Malcolm said. "I hope you live for a week." He gave the other boy a push. The boy with a hole in his middle fell backward.

Malcolm rummaged in his pocket and found a knife. He cut Rudge's hands loose. It was several minutes before Rudge trusted his throbbing, burning hands to pick up his Colts. His hands and feet felt as if they were afire. His hip felt as if the furies were bound inside it, struggling to get out. And the lightning seemed to have done something else to him. He felt dazed, as if this was not all really happening.

He stared at the boy who writhed at his feet, still making that funny sobbing, sucking sound with each labored breath.

"You all right?" Malcolm asked. "Think you can walk?"

Rudge nodded.

"You jus' goin' to leave me here to die?"

"I suppose I could shoot you," Rudge said wearily.

"Not on your tintype!" Malcolm snapped. He turned to the writhing horse thief. "What was it you was plannin' for me, Opie?"

"Hurts. Oooooooh, it hurts."

"Bet it hurts near as much as breakin' in a pair of crooked shoes," Malcolm said. He turned his back on the dying horse thief and fashioned a torch from the remnants of the fire. He got one of Rudge's arms over his shoulder and began helping him up the hill. "Don't shoot, Aggie," he yelled and for an instant his voice slipped back into a boyish soprano. "It's me and Mr. Rudge acomin' in."

This isn't really happening, Rudge told himself. It's just another dream—another memory. But as he limped and stumbled uphill with Malcolm's help, he knew it was happening, that behind him in the darkness a boy lay noisily dying. He didn't feel right about it. Mainly he was shamed that he had botched a job and forced a mere boy to clean up after him. "I'm sorry," he muttered.

"For what?" the Maclendon boy asked.

"For not killing him when I had a chance."

"Why, I'd've been plumb put out," Malcolm said. "Been wantin' to do that ever since he shot my dog."

Rudge sighed, knowing it had always been this way. Getting old, he told himself. If he didn't watch it, soon he would be maundering on about the good old days.

"*¡Alto! ¡Párale ahí!*" It sounded like Mrs. Lowery.

They halted. "It's us, Aggie," the boy repeated. "Mr. Rudge and me."

"*¿Están solos?*"

It was a reasonable precaution, Rudge supposed, for her to ask if they were alone. After all, that moaning and squirming wretch down in the meadow had been planning on using one or both of them to force his way into camp. Then he saw a deeper meaning in her question. Mrs. Lowery must know the penny-farthing riders did not speak Spanish.

Suddenly Rudge felt slightly better about it all. The Maclendons were not lying. They had been here first, been here long enough to learn the customs and language of the country. What right had a bunch of newcomers to push them off their range—even if the one living God did happen to prefer cows to sheep?

Speaking in Spanish, both Rudge and the boy assured Mrs. Lowery that they were alone, that they were not under duress, and that she was to shoot only at whoever might present himself behind the man and boy who staggered drunkenly uphill bearing a pine torch.

They reached the hilltop and struggled over the barrels and sacks into the "fort." Rudge was so undone that he found himself stretched out on a damp blanket beneath the tarp that stretched from one upended buckboard to the other before he realized he had not checked his Colts.

While Malcolm gabbled with his sister and the old woman just as boyishly as if he had not just killed another boy, Rudge went over his guns by the stub of a candle.

There was a scratch on the butt of one. Nothing that couldn't be polished out with patience and a mutton bone. He cleaned them, oiled them, and checked the mechanism for looseness. Finally he decided the dying boy had done no real damage. "Did the lightning bother you up here?" he finally asked.

"No, Mr. Rudge. Did it strike close to you down there?"

"Exceeding close," he said, and tried to wish away the numbing tingle in his limbs.

It was puzzling. Why had the lightning struck down a tree in the meadow instead of hitting the hilltop up here? But there were other more urgent mysteries in this country. "Did you ever shoot any of those people downstream?" he asked.

From brother and sister's shocked surprise Rudge knew they had not. "We are not barbarians, Mr. Rudge," the redhead said reprovingly.

"I was not suggesting you were." He tried to put from his mind the faint sounds of anguish that still rose from the meadow below. "It's just that I can't help wondering why people with so few cattle and plenty of grass have such an obsession with Maclendon sheep."

"You heard what he called me," Malcolm said.

The younger Maclendon seemed to have discharged the curse that had lain upon him since the deaths of his brother-in-law and his father. Rudge was at a loss to understand it.

As long as he had been omnipotent, a perfect figure for a boy's hero worship, young Malcolm had been standoffish; no doubt at least partly because of that note he had written the sheriff to get the boy out of his way.

But now that Rudge had been humiliated and demonstrated to be as prone to failure as any other man, Malcolm had warmed to him. Was it really possible that the three of them could relax up here in the cool aftermath of the rain, sitting and gabbing just as if nobody could hear the sobbing and gasping that continued unabated?

That horse thief was dead and just didn't know it. Rudge
had known the instant he had seen which way the boy bent
over. But the small-bore slug from a saloon pistol had little
shock value. The boy might, as Malcolm cheerfully hoped,
live for a week.

"*Si fuera caballo—*" the old woman muttered.

"But he ain't a horse," Malcolm countered. "No horse
ever spent all his time workin' out ways to do me dirty."

"But on the other hand, he never had your advantages,"
Mrs. Lowery said placatingly. She turned to Rudge whose
aches were forcing him to use every bit of his willpower not
to moan as loudly as the dying boy. "What do you think,
Mr. Rudge?"

"We've already seen the results of my misguided mercy,"
he said. "Had I obeyed my instincts earlier today none of this
might have happened."

"But don't you believe that wretched creature is at least
as deserving of kindness as a broken-legged horse?"

Rudge was hurting in too many places to shrug. "But who
shall bell the cat?" he asked.

Mrs. Lowery sighed and began a painful rise to her feet.
"If you'll lend me one of your pistols," she began.

"I'll do it," Malcolm offered.

"You'll enjoy it," Mrs. Lowery protested.

Rudge was hurting so bad it was difficult for him to care
much which of them did it. He should have done it himself.

Malcolm shrugged. "What difference does it make?
Wouldn't you get a kick out of doin' in one of them as did in
Paw?" He tried to make himself comfortable in the limited
dry space under the tarp. "'Sides," he added, "if you're
talkin' fun, I'd ruther listen. That's what poor sufferin' Opie
was plannin' for me."

"For all of us, I'm afraid," Rudge added. "I've never been
sure whether it's bravery, foolhardiness, or cowardice that
makes us let avowed enemies live."

There was a long silence as each of them pondered the

distance to civilization and the ease with which they could shed its restraints. Down in the darkness the gut-shot boy was moaning for a mercy he had never offered.

Rudge had heard that sound before when bivouacked where neither side had dared go out to tend their wounded. He could think of pleasanter sounds to lull him to sleep. While the three of them pondered the gulf between what should be done and the act of doing it the moaning was punctuated by a sudden shriek. "No!" the boy howled. "Please!" Then abruptly there were no more complaints.

Moments later there was a mumbled, *"No me tiren; soy Rosaura."* The old woman came into camp.

In his agony Rudge had not even noticed she was gone. From their surprise it would seem none of the others had noted the old woman's absence either. They stared at the bloody knife that the old woman matter-of-factly began cleaning.

"Un cabrón menos," she said.

The old woman had gone to the heart of the problem. In a war of extermination, "one less cuckold" was an improvement in the odds. He reminded himself that his introduction to this valley had been a burning shepherd's caravan with this old woman's dead husband beside it. At least one person around here understood the situation. Two, he amended as he remembered Malcolm.

"You're unwell, Mr. Rudge," the redhead said.

"You have the Scots gift for understatement," he managed.

Without comment she produced the Green River. She poured generous doses for Rudge and Malcolm, then settled down with the old woman to wait out and dry out.

"Hope *you're* feeling better," Rudge said as the whiskey began to soak in.

"No doubt better than you," she said.

Daylight came and apart from a few dampnesses in sheltered spots it might never have rained. The creek had gone down to its normal trickle and the long-suffering horses were where Rudge had tied them last night when he heard the shots. He forced himself to stand and stump about inside the fort until the first bright edge of agony departed. He decided that no permanent damage had been done. More importantly, he resolved that never ever again would he attribute more importance to somebody else's life than to his own comfort. Never, at least, until he had attained an age where life was no longer important.

"We ought to bury him," Mrs. Lowery said.

"He didn't want me breathin' his air," Malcolm said flatly. "I don't want him pollutin' Maclendon ground."

She looked at Rudge.

"I'm afraid I'm in no shape even to bury my friends," he apologized.

They were silent, thinking not so much of the proprieties as of more mundane consequences. Soon there would be coyotes, vultures, flies, a contaminated water supply. Rudge remembered the holeful of explosives downstream that had almost blown him up. But he was too bruised and aching even to think of riding that far.

"I could take him," Malcolm offered.

"And get caught down there alone?" Mrs. Lowery snapped. "By the way, where were you yesterday?"

"Went to see how Eusebio and the others were holding out."

"And?"

The boy shrugged. "The trouble all seems to center here. Nobody's bothered them much."

Cut off the head and the members wither, Rudge supposed. And in any event, the Maclendon headquarters were within easier striking distance than were scattered herds and shepherds.

He glanced up and saw Mrs. Lowery studying him. "Is there any other way?" she asked.

"Apart from extermination?"

She nodded. "I can't understand it. Father lived through

Indian troubles. I don't suppose anyone was ever softheaded enough to think him a kind man. But the Maclendons have always been just. We did not go out of our way to make enemies."

"Well," Rudge sighed, "you have them. 'Twould appear that it's a question of you or them."

"And to think that we're living in the nineteenth century!" she sniffed.

"We live in an age of marvels," Rudge said. "Ironclad warships, repeating rifles, Gatling guns, shrapnel, torpedoes, and dynamite."

XVIII

"How many do you suppose are left?" Mrs. Lowery asked.

"Penny-farthings?"

"Whatever you choose to call them."

Rudge pondered. The morning he had gone down there he had been astonished at how few and how runted the cattle. Unless the men were stacked like cordwood inside that bunkhouse—"Couldn't have been over a baker's dozen to start with," he said. "And we've picked off a few. They might still have eight effectives."

"Against three of us."

"Two of you. I shall no doubt recover within a few days."

"Ummmm yes," Mrs. Lowery said thoughtfully. She got to her feet and bustled around sweeping the damp ground between the upended buckboards. With rain to soften it and their tramping to pound it down the dirt promised to turn hard as wellmade adobe. "Out of water again," she said brightly, and sent her brother and Rosaura down to the stream with canteens and a packhorse.

"I can take care of it," Malcolm protested.

"Both of you," Mrs. Lowery said firmly. "Somebody should keep watch. Also," she added, "you might put a shovelful of dirt over that—untidiness—to keep down the flies."

Grumbling and muttering, Malcolm and Rosaura went downhill toward the creek.

"The coast is clear," Mrs. Lowery said after they had departed.

Rudge rose painfully to his elbow and looked downstream. "So it would appear," he said. It was only when he lay back down and saw the peculiarly intent look on the redhead's face that he understood what she was talking about. Of all the Goddamn times!

"I ache in every joint and fissure," he explained, "save those where mortification has set in. At the very least I shall require a week's rest and several hot baths."

Mrs. Lowery turned nearly as red as her hair. "Nor am I at my best," she admitted when she had gotten hold of herself again. "And in any event, what you suggest has its time and place—neither of which are here. I want you to examine my wound."

"I'm not a physician."

"Nor am I, nor anyone else in the immediate vicinity. If I expose myself to Rosaura I shall be immediately smeared with dung to drive out demons. You seem to have heard of Lister and antisepsis."

"What can I do for you?"

"My wound itches most abominably. I cannot see it. Please tell me if it needs lancing to let out morbid matter."

When Rudge nodded she gave a final glance downhill and scooted around to sit with her back to where he lay. She undid her shirtwaist and took it off, affording Rudge a rear exposure of arms and shoulders in no way deficient from any others he had seen. She worked her petticoat off one shoulder and, blushing furiously, exposed a red swollen streak beneath her left armpit.

"May I touch it?" he asked.

She did not speak but nodded, her fair skin turning a more vivid shade of red. Rudge put out his hand, then touched the other side for comparison. He lay back down on his blanket.

"Well?" she demanded.

"Looks fine to me. Give me a week and I shall be delighted to subject you to a more thoroughgoing examination."

Mrs. Lowery chose not to hear this. "No mortification?" she demanded.

"None. In a week you may be treating me."

In less time than he would have imagined possible, Mrs. Lowery had her shirtwaist back on and sat across the confined space as far as possible from him. She would not look in his direction. "Mr. Rudge," she finally asked, "what are we going to do?"

Rudge considered the several possible answers to this question and hesitated. "I should fancy our principal concern at the moment is to survive," he said. "Since the sheriff seems unwilling or unable to invoke the forces of law and order, we are reduced to elemental methods."

From her sigh he suspected that Mrs. Lowery had been waiting for Rudge to address himself to a totally different problem. Why was it, he wondered, that women never got these ideas in their heads as long as a man was rested, well fed, and enjoying reasonable health? But just let a man get to hurting and . . . maybe it was some bit of internal piping that cross-connected between procreative and maternal instincts. Down and out as he was feeling right now, Rudge was going to have to watch out lest in a moment of weakness he commit himself to terms above and beyond one third of a rapidly shrinking estate. He was spared further questioning by the return of Rosaura and Malcolm and a horse festooned with water bags and canteens. "Get it off your chest?" the boy asked.

Rudge closed his eyes and pretended to sleep while Mrs. Lowery tried not to overdo her outrage. He wondered if he would ever be finished with aching. But even as Malcolm and his sister bickered to the amusement of the old woman, Rudge lay with his eyes closed and tried to decide what, after all, they were all going to do.

There seemed no choice in the matter. As soon as he was able to sit a horse without howling he would have to get back down there to the penny-farthings—kill a few, improve the odds for the decimated Maclendons.

He was not as bad off as he had been. *Un cabrón menos,* as Rosaura had put it: one less cuckold down there in the meadow. And one more gun up here. After last night he would never again take Malcolm for an untried boy. He had thought they stopped making boys like that in 1865.

He squinted at the sun through half-opened eyes. Early morning. Another long day ahead. If he didn't stop taking a new rap every day he was never going to recruit from the aches and pains that had been multiplying since first a bullet had creased his scalp and then a stirrup had whacked him on the thigh. All he needed now was a full-scale invasion of the penny-farthings. He closed his eyes, took a deep breath, and prayed they would not come before he had found time to recover. Just as he closed his eyes Mrs. Lowery said, "Oh dear!"

Without opening his eyes, Rudge checked his pockets for fresh ammunition. He felt his newly cleaned Colts. "How many?" he asked. "And how long before they're in range?"

Even as he said it he knew he was indulging in the kind of carelessness that could kill him. "Does the rifle shoot where it points?" he asked, "or must one indulge its little niceties?"

"Shoots straight if you 'low for windage," Malcolm said. "You a good shot with a Springfield?"

Abruptly Rudge remembered that Mrs. Lowery had said the boy was a crack shot with this weapon.

"We may not be using it," the redhead said. "I don't believe those are Double-O riders."

So that was the proper term for the penny-farthings.

"Who are they?" the boy demanded.

"I believe it's Sheriff Jason," Mrs. Lowery said. "But this time he's not alone."

"I'm sorry, Mrs. Lowery," Rudge said.

"Over what?"

"If I could ride," he explained, "I'd go downstream and massacre a few penny-farthings first."

"First?"

"Before the sheriff and his *posse comitatus* of law-abiding Soda Springs citizens could get around to massacring me."

"Oh?"

"You'd best not fight them," he continued. "No use spreading your war onto two fronts."

"And give up the better part of my army?" Mrs. Lowery snapped. She turned to peer past the upended buckboard. "I don't believe it's a posse anyway," she reported. "If it is, you'll find it insultingly small."

Rudge grasped the perch of the buckboard and dragged himself laboriously to his feet. "It seems more to resemble those banker chaps who offered to buy you out," he said.

The sheriff and his companions rode into the clearing and seemed puzzled for a moment. Rudge wondered why. Even if the sheriff had not been here before, the two bankers would have told him about the burnout. Then he saw they had finally spotted the body of the boy whose life Rudge had been at such pains to save.

Rudge winced and struggled to find some comfortable position. Comfort, he suspected, lay at least a quiet week in the future.

"Rudge!" the sheriff yelled.

To hell with him! Let the old man work it out for himself.

"Miz Lowery, you still got that Reb up there?"

"So nice of you to come, Sheriff!" the redhead called back. "Are we finally to have law and order in this valley?"

"That depends on whether you're gonna keep on harborin' a fugitive," the sheriff called back. Behind him the two bankers silently sat their horses. When nobody from the hilltop replied, Sheriff Jason added, "This time 'tain't just some thirsty freighter. Is a banker a good enough witness for you?"

Malcolm and Mrs. Lowery readied their weapons. Neither seemed able to meet Rudge's eyes.

"I don't believe it," Malcolm grumped.

Finally Agnes Lowery faced Rudge. "You are in pain?" she asked. Obviously, she could not bring herself to ask the question that was on her mind. "Is there anything I can do for you?"

"You might fetch me some corn pone and a mint julep."

Mrs. Lowery gasped and seemed diminished. After an instant of hesitation she managed a "Thank you, Mr. Rudge."

"You said you was English," Malcolm accused.

"I cannot recall ever making such a statement."

"You said it dozens of times!"

"If you'd listened carefully you'd've discovered that I attended school in England. The same may be said for Arabs, East Indians, and Hottentots."

"But—"

"But, being totally unreconstructed, I swear no false oaths, pledge no hypocritical allegiance to an oppressor's flag. I give you Joseph Bentley Rudge. I am what I am."

"But you do give us that," Mrs. Lowery said flatly. "And this hardly seems the moment for a crisis of conscience."

"Your vision is remarkably untainted by wishful thinking," Rudge said. "And now what shall we do about those who remain undecided?"

"I hadn't thought of it that way," Mrs. Lowery said, and managed a hint of a smile. She put private disappointments behind her. Stretching until she could look over the upended buckboard, she called, "Sheriff! Your fence-straddling days are over. Declare yourself."

"Aggie, I don't know what you're talkin' about. You got that Reb up there or not?"

"I'm talking about your responsibility to the electorate. Are you with us or against us? That piece of vermin at your feet was against us. If you can't keep trash from annoying decent people, then you might as well earn your wages burying him."

"Don't you dare go poisonin' Maclendon land!" Malcolm added. "You git him downstream away from here!"

"You ain't makin' it any better for yourself talkin' that way," the sheriff called back. "Now you gonna let me come up there peaceable—or are you gonna make me earn my pay?"

Rudge wondered how the old man could be so wrongheaded. Could he still truly believe the Maclendons had started this war? Rudge sighed and checked his Colts, trying to ignore the pain that suffused his every movement. He caught at the perch of the upended buckboard and drew himself cautiously to his feet. The sheriff and the pair of bankers still grouped together near the body at the bottom of the hill. Too close for men who had fought for the Union and were supposed to know something of tactics. Even at this range he suspected that he could pick off the three of them with no more than three shots.

The sheriff ought to know it too. Obviously, the old man was counting on long acquaintance to stay the Maclendon hand. "You comin' down or do I have to come up?" he called.

"Don't kill him," Rudge muttered, "or you're truly finished in this country."

"I know that, Mr. Rudge," the redhead snapped. "But what do you suggest I do?"

"I'm comin' up now, Aggie," the sheriff called. "And you better be ready to hand that Reb over."

"The war's been over for ten years," she yelled.

"War ain't never over for murderers didn't even wear uniforms. I'm comin' up now."

"Plenty of sand in his craw for such an old man," Malcolm said grudgingly.

"Let him come," Rudge said.

"Don't kill him!" It was Mrs. Lowery.

"That was not my intention," Rudge said.

"You gonna let him take you?" Malcolm asked.

From the corner of the fort the old woman watched from ancient eyes that saw all and told nothing.

Rudge stood until his *sevillano* was unmistakable above the upended buckboard. "Come on up, Sheriff!" he called. "Bring your friends with you. Step lively now. You have the word of Joseph Bentley Rudge that I'll not shoot you."

"Guilty conscience, Mr. Rudge?" The redhead's tone was withering.

Rudge sighed. "You told me once that the whole country was choosing up sides." He pointed.

Malcolm and his sister stared. "Oh!" Mrs. Lowery managed.

XIX

"You're wasting time," Rudge yelled down at the sheriff. "Bring your weapons if you wish, but stop dithering. Just get up here before I change my lawless and mercurial mind."

The bankers' nervousness transmitted itself to their horses and it was a full minute before the trio sorted out their prancing beasts and began urging them uphill.

"Don't point guns," Rudge murmured to Malcolm and Mrs. Lowery. "Do you want to force them to the other side?"

"But Mr. Rudge, should we let them up here?"

Rudge pointed downstream. "Don't you believe it wise that we prevent three more undecided guns from joining with that lot?"

Mrs. Lowery bit her lips. Malcolm saw to his weapons.

From the hilltop they had a more inclusive view of the country than was available to the sheriff and his companions down in the valley floor. Rudge studied the trio as their horses slipped and skittered uphill. There was a moment of awkwardness as they approached the final few yards but finally the sheriff and bankers saw Rudge's holstered Colts. Gradually it seeped into their edginess that he had no intention of drawing on them. They were tying their mounts to upended buckboard wheels when Rudge suggested, "Best turn them loose."

The sheriff's eyes narrowed. "We ain't plannin' on stayin' all that long."

"Perhaps not," Rudge said. "But when the shooting starts

your mustangs will surely panic. Even if they're not shot they'll pull the fort apart and leave us all exposed."

"Exposed to what?"

Rudge smiled. "Welcome to our faction," he said. "The days of your fine-honed impartiality have just ended."

"You seem to think I didn't come up here to arrest you." Cautiously, the sheriff drew his single Peacemaker and pointed it at Rudge.

"I'm sure that was your original purpose," Rudge said. Malcolm and the redhead waited in rigid silence, still gripping their weapons but not threatening anyone. "Just as my original purpose was to pass quietly through this country on my lawful private business," Rudge sighed. "But your inability or unwillingness to preserve law and order forced a change in my plans."

"I come up here to change them again," the sheriff began.

Rudge took a deep breath and tried not to dwell on how much he ached. "Life," he philosophized, "is largely a matter of how the chickens come home to roost. Had you done what needed to be done at the proper time, none of this might have happened."

"Can't you ever talk straight?"

"Straighter than is your liking," Rudge said. "Look downstream and you'll see an ample number of chickens heading this way." With a movement smooth and totally unexpected, Rudge drew one Colt and snapped a shot off at the approaching raiders. His pistol was back in its holster before the sheriff had time to realize how easily the shot could have been aimed at him. "And that precludes any thought of talking your way out of this one. Welcome to the godly host."

Glumly, the sheriff and his companions looked downstream. There were more penny-farthings than Rudge had expected. He counted a dozen horses, but only eleven men. One horse bore twin panniers draped from a sawbuck packsaddle. Rudge sighed. The penny-farthings seemed determined to camp long enough to starve them out. Or at least until they ran out of water.

He studied the supply of canteens and jugs. Without horses they could have held out for a week—until the sheriff and bankers came to add to their problems.

The raiders were well supplied, outnumbered them, and had the creek to drink from. They dismounted and began taking positions. "A rifle," Rudge said. He took his time aiming at one of the pair who were dragging the dead boy out of sight. The Springfield boomed and the kick renewed every half-dormant ache and twinge in his abused body. The bullet stirred dust beyond the man he had shot at. Rudge swallowed his disgust and wondered if the sights were off or if he had made the usual mistake shooting downhill. Should have let the boy try it.

By the time he had ejected the shell and reloaded, the penny-farthings were dug in. A shot whistled high over the fort. Rudge looked at the sun. Still hours short of noon. "We're in for a long wait," he predicted. "They'll not charge this position by daylight." He sighed and handed the rifle to Malcolm. Turning to the sheriff and the bankers, he said, "I'm really not at my best today. Call me if anything happens."

The white-eyed one who had thought he recognized Rudge opened his eyes wider but did not speak. Still, Rudge's hopes were not realized. The others were all talking at cross purposes, each too intent on what he was saying to listen to anyone else's equally momentous pronunciamentos.

"It's him," the banker whose name he had never learned was insisting. "I wasn't sure before but I am now."

"Looks like they all got rifles," the sheriff was saying.

"If you'd stood on your own two legs six months ago, you wouldn't be trapped up here to die with us," Mrs. Lowery snapped.

"If old Bull Oostenveld sticks his head up anywhere, you just leave him to me," Malcolm instructed.

"*Son los mismos que nos quemaron la casa,*" old Rosaura said.

The older banker—Tedrow—seemed to be the only one listening. "These are the same lot that burnt down the ranch?" he echoed.

"*Y mataron a mi viejo,*" she added.

Tedrow raised his hat. "I'm truly sorry to know they killed your husband," he said. To himself he added, "And even sorrier to know they'll probably kill me. Why did I ever get into this?"

"You could not resist a bargain," Rudge said.

The banker turned to Rudge. "Are you—" he began. "Is it true that you rode with Quantrill's Raiders?"

The several disparate monologues came to an abrupt end as everyone looked down at Rudge. "Were you with Sherman in Georgia?" Rudge countered. "Your partner's face bears a remarkable resemblance to posters inquiring into the whereabouts of a Jesse James. Now the sheriff over there looks rather like General Wirz of infamous memory. And those scoundrels down by the creek look determined to kill us all without cavil over which rajah or emperor claimed our loyalties."

"Were you?" Mrs. Lowery asked.

"I'm a secret agent for the tsar!" Rudge snapped. "On my way to conquer San Francisco."

"*¡Que nos asista!*" the old woman muttered.

"Who?" the sheriff asked.

"San Francisco, of course," Rudge said. "And I pray the good St. Francis arrives well supplied with water and ammunition."

The sheriff had been poking about in their confined space, bounded on two sides by upturned buckboards and on the other two by the barrels and crates Rudge had freighted in. He picked up the gold pan from Rudge's kit. "You ain't no miner; that's for sure."

Suddenly both bankers were very interested in the gold

pan. The sheriff held it out to them. "Where's the rust?" he asked, and ran a finger over its greasy inner surface. "Either it ain't never been burnt clean or else he's usin' it to fry fatback. Ain't nobody gonna pan gold with that."

"Has anyone ever reported gold in this country?" Rudge asked.

Tedrow and his nameless wide-eyed partner gave Rudge an odd look, then quickly looked away. And suddenly Rudge knew the name of the game. "The price just went up to thirty thousand," he said.

"You're mad!" the nameless one snapped.

"Perhaps," Rudge admitted. "But I'm also tired, in some pain, and would like to order my soul for what promises to be an interesting night. Please try to limit your sordid haggling." He found his Green River, upended it, and killed the bottle. Bankers and sheriff were still muttering furiously when he dropped off to sleep. He was half-roused periodically by the sound of a shot whistling overhead.

It was afternoon when Rudge awoke feeling as if a squadron of household cavalry had stood parade in his mouth. He was, if anything, more afflicted with aches than before. But now the pain in his hip was mitigated by a headache.

The others sat glum and red-eyed, crowded beneath the tarp to escape the sun. In one corner the old woman was pounding a string of dried red chiles into powder.

"Still haven't found any way to desert us and change sides?" Rudge asked cheerfully. "I'd've thought you'd be down there and shooting up at us by now. By the way, how did you ever make the acquaintance of Mr. Lowery? Seems odd that two bankers from way down in Santa Fe would come up here on a wild-goose chase just because some stranger wrote a letter. Or does your profession receive a constant supply of this sort of pig-in-a-poke offers?"

"Really, Mr. Rudge, I see no cause for levity."

"Nor I, Mrs. Lowery, but we gladiators are always more

cheerful once we understand the forces which impel us to our fates. *Morituri te salutamus* and all that rot."

"We all know you ain't no Englishman," the sheriff growled. "Now why can't you talk American for a change?"

"Actually it was Latin," Rudge said. "We who are about to die salute you, as Caesar's hired killers were taught to greet him." He paused and wished for another bottle of Green River. "Tell me," he began, "is there a single martyr in this camp who wouldn't welcome the chance to throw away his share in exchange for his life?"

Mrs. Lowery gave him an anxious look. "Are you well, Mr. Rudge?" she asked. "What shares are you talking about?"

"Shares in the gold mine your husband was selling," Rudge said airily. "Surely you don't expect a pair of banking magnates from a metropolis like Santa Fe to come stampeding up here all this distance braving indigent Indians and hostile whites just to invest in a floundering sheep ranch?

"Thirty thousand, did I say?" He turned to Tedrow and the nameless man who accused him. "Here's your chance to die rich. But the claim appreciates while you ponder the offer. The price is now thirty-two thousand, five hundred."

"You might try getting him out of the sun," Tedrow said dryly.

"Thirty-five thousand and going up," Rudge chanted. "You may be able to sweet-talk Malcolm and Mrs. Lowery into selling their thirds for less but my price is thirty-five thousand and rising."

"*Your* price?"

"Surely you don't think I'd settle for a paltry third of nothing—not after all those test holes and assay work!"

Malcolm gasped. "So that's why there was nobody in the gravel!"

"Correct the first time," Rudge said. "Mr. Lowery was not selling a sheep ranch. He was offering a gold mine. The prospects were so good that those penny-farthings—Oostenvelds or whatever you choose to call them—lazy rotters can't even take proper care of their few head of cattle, and yet someone has great expectations—great enough to dig the foundations and plan a palace behind that one-room shanty of a great house."

He turned to Malcolm and Mrs. Lowery. "They'll spend the afternoon trying to explain to you the speculative nature of gold mining, that they're putting all their money into a will-of-the-wisp. Before you sign anything, remember that the price of my third just went up to thirty-seven thousand, five hundred. And now please try to limit your squabbling. I am tired, out of sorts, and I suspect my peculiar talents are about to be in demand come sundown." He rolled up in his blanket and did his best to ignore the hornet's nest he had stirred up.

They wrangled. They raved. They shouted at one another. Tedrow was silent but the other banker struggled to assure Mrs. Lowery that nobody had even hinted at the existence of gold in this valley. Sheriff Jason squatted in one corner of the fort with a quizzical expression, studying the lot of them, looking from time to time at a resting Rudge whose *sevillano* was drawn over his face.

Downhill the penny-farthings finished digging in. They were in no hurry. Every ten or fifteen minutes a shot would come into the camp. After one punctured a water bag the old woman and Malcolm got the rest of them in and out of sight.

Most of the raiders' shots went overhead. Rudge drowsed and remembered how difficult it was to aim properly uphill or down. Somebody down there ought to be bracketing, getting the range with a single weapon instead of this sporadic popping. Then finally he realized what they were trying to do. The penny-farthings must believe all that folklore about lost bullets. They were shooting howitzer-fashion into the sky and hoping to get over the fort's walls by hitting their targets on the drop. "Put your hats on," Rudge suggested.

"One of those slugs raps you, it could give you a headache."

"'Druther give one of them a headache," Malcolm muttered. He had been poised on his knees, aiming the Springfield through a hole in the buckboard bed for several minutes now. Finally he fired. There was a howl from downhill.

"Looks like you did it," the sheriff said. "Now if you could just give the other ten of them a headache, I could arrest your lime-juice friend here and get back into town."

XX

Rudge found a water bag and helped himself. "Puts you in a difficult position, doesn't it, Sheriff?" he asked.

"How?"

"You need my firepower. On the other hand, there's not the slightest constraint on my criminal mind—nothing to keep me from potting you and your odd, purportedly banker friends in the back, side, or front. But should you kill me—even if you were to survive whatever's planned for the lot of us at sundown, you might get back to civilization and discover you'd killed the wrong man. And if you think the Alabama claims stirred up a tempest, just fancy what future awaits you once the United States Government discovers you've murdered a blameless British subject and destroyed the Union's case."

"You ain't no Limey."

"Nor are you a competent authority. Ask your banker friends how they first made acquaintance with the late Mr. Lowery."

"I don't see what that's got to do with it."

"If I were enforcing the law, I'd want to know everything about a case. Or at the very least, I'd copper my bets enough to forestall the grand jury that's sure to come stampeding in here and overrunning this place just like Sutter's Mill."

Mrs. Lowery gasped.

"Yes," Rudge said. "And don't think it won't happen. I'm amazed that pack of scoundrels downhill managed to keep it to themselves as long as they did."

"But my father—"

"Was a sheepman," Rudge concluded. "No more interested in seeing his quiet and prosperous life disrupted by gold-hungry strangers than was the unfortunate founder of Nueva Helvecia. I understand that poor Sutter is still, after twenty-five years, seeking compensation for damages to his estate from a totally deaf and uncaring Congress."

"What's that got to do with you?" the nameless banker demanded. "You're wanted for riding with Quantrill."

"On your testimony?"

"Mine and others'."

"Are the others also convicted felons? Surely even our provincial sheriff understands the limitations on the testimony of convicts."

Tedrow was regarding his partner with increasing distaste.

"I'll put my record against yours any day!" the younger banker blazed. "I'm no convict!"

"Not yet," Rudge said. "But once the statutes for fraud are duly enforced, then where will you be?"

"What on earth are you talking about, Mr. Rudge?" It was Mrs. Lowery.

"About obtaining your land under false pretenses. Surely you've noted how these— A consideration for your sex prohibits me from employing the proper term for the sort of scavenger who was heading this way to pick up the pieces before your father was even dead."

"Please"—Tedrow interrupted—"I am employed to protect other people's investments. Had I known what was going on here, I certainly would have recommended most emphatically that our bank stay out."

"Then what are you doing here?" Rudge demanded.

"Throwing good money after bad, I fear." Tedrow turned to his nameless companion. "Stanley, perhaps you could tell me what I'm doing here."

"You're not laying it on me," Stanley said flatly. "I told

you everything I knew at the time and you approved the deal." The formerly nameless banker turned to Rudge. "You're the reason I came back."

Rudge grinned. "Had you displayed enough intelligence to stay away, you might have no need of my firepower."

"Firepower hell!" Stanley snapped, then turned pink as he faced Mrs. Lowery. "Sorry, ma'am. It was Mr. Lowery led me into this."

The redhead studied the banker with a puzzled air. "As a banker you must receive astonishing propositions every day. How ever did Mr. Lowery's letters induce you to travel this distance?"

"You might say he was a friend of mine."

"Might?" Rudge asked.

Stanley threw up his hands. "What difference does it make now? They're going to kill us all anyhow."

"The difference is whether you hang me or I hang you once we've disposed of those scoundrels below," Rudge said. "Now tell us about Mr. Lowery."

"Yes," Tedrow added. "That's a story I'd enjoy hearing too."

Stanley looked at Mrs. Lowery and raised his hands.

"Perhaps you fear to offend me with the knowledge that my husband was a scoundrel?" the redhead asked. "I believe even our totally wrongheaded sheriff will agree to that."

Stanley shrugged. He scrunched about to make himself comfortable with his back against the upended buckboard. A spent bullet thunked against the weathered wood and he struggled to make himself smaller. "Lowery and I served together," he began. "From sixty-two to late sixty-four. I wasn't very old then. He sort of looked out for me. Wasn't till I got a little older that I started noticing how much I was paying for his friendship."

Against her will Mrs. Lowery emitted a short bark of laughter.

"You couldn't ask for a more likeable man," Stanley continued. "He was a regular jimdandy. But there was always something big coming along—something going to make us both rich if I could just come up with enough money to—"

"Welcome to the club," Rudge said.

"He was a most convincing man," Mrs. Lowery agreed. "How much did you contribute toward your own education?"

"Fifteen hundred dollars," Stanley confessed.

Several listeners whistled.

"My mother's homestead," the banker explained. "And it almost worked. Would have if we'd just had another couple of hundred to tide us over."

"You can't blow off a good mark," Rudge murmured.

"I beg your pardon?"

"A sucker," Rudge explained, "never knows he's been trimmed. A good confidence man makes it all look like a run of bad luck. He rides off into the sunset with a victim's money and the sucker waves farewell without the slightest thought of revenge. Done properly, the mark thinks, 'Poor Harry lost even worse than I. Perhaps someday we can get together again and make it pan out the next time.'"

Stanley was staring at Rudge, showing entirely too much white of eye.

"So Mr. Lowery approached you after all these years and offered to win back all your losses, providing you could just put up a little front money. Correct me if I'm wrong."

"It would have worked," Stanley snapped. "It can still work. This is valuable land. There's enough gold here to finance another war."

"Looks like it's already financing one," the sheriff said with a glance downhill.

Tedrow sighed and looked at his younger partner. "And on the strength of this you committed our bank—?"

"Any of you people ever actually dug gold?" the sheriff asked.

Rudge stared intently at the graying lawman. "A penny for your thoughts," he offered, "and a full ration of base metal for voicing them."

The sheriff glanced at Rudge's Colts and took in his meaning. He raised his eyebrows slightly. "Plenty of time to deal with you," he said.

"It's all nonsense," Mrs. Lowery said. "My husband had not visited the ranch for months before his death. He couldn't have done any digging."

"He didn't," Rudge explained. "Someone put a bug in your father's ear. He dug one hole and quietly filled it in again once he had learned what he wished to know—and what he wished the rest of the world not to know."

"Oh dear!" Mrs. Lowery gasped.

"It's real!" Malcolm exulted. "Money to get out of this god-awful country!"

"Unfortunately," Rudge added, "the word somehow filtered down to the Oostenvelds. Possibly it filtered down quite literally in the form of muddied water from panning and sluicing. In any event, what I assumed was some diabolically well-planned trap for me was nothing of the sort. I set fire accidentally to someone's cache of blasting powder."

Tedrow threw up his hands. "Why did I travel all the way from Santa Fe to get in on the ground floor of some scheme that seems to be common knowledge? By the way, is there any gold here?"

Rudge shrugged. "When one considers the ends everyone went to in covering up their test holes and keeping mum—"

Tedrow turned to Mrs. Lowery and Malcolm who sat side by side next to old Rosaura. "Did any of you know there was gold here?"

"*¿Qué dice?*" the old woman demanded.

"*Que si sabíamos que hay oro por acá.*"

"*Locos,*" she muttered and turned her attention inward.

"I'm afraid we're all equally victims," Tedrow sighed. "In any event, Mrs. Lowery, my bank is not interested in get-rich-quick schemes. Assuming all or any of us get out of here alive, the bank's original offer of twenty thousand stands. However, my personal recommendation is that you double or triple your money elsewhere. I am bound by the original tender but I have no intent of raising it."

"How odd," Rudge murmured.

"I beg your pardon?"

"An honest banker. Almost enough to make one take literally all that rot about passing through the eye of a needle."

Tedrow turned the color of a new brick but stood his ground. "I make a comfortable living without trimming widows and orphans," he snapped.

"I'll give you sixty thousand!" It was his partner, Stanley.

"Mine and my brother's shares?" the redhead asked. "Or do you include Mr. Rudge's?"

"I'll get his by escheat," Stanley assured her.

"You assume," Rudge said icily, "that legal murder will not be avenged by my family and my sovereign queen. Even if they were remiss in their duties, the law forbids a murderer to profit from his crime. In addition, if I read Mr. Maclendon's will correctly, the other heirs cannot sell their shares without my approval. Which of my boots would you care to lick first?"

"There's a thousand-dollar reward out for you," Stanley muttered.

"Puts you in a fix, doesn't it? You can make a thousand dollars by throwing away perhaps a hundred times that much." Abruptly Rudge remembered something else. "By the way, Sheriff, I'm still waiting for the official word on any reward for those scoundrels I delivered to you last week."

"You've got your gall!" the sheriff growled.

"Also two converted Colts and a knowledge of my worth. Unless we reach an agreement you and your friends may as well join the other side." Lest any of them consider this course of action, Rudge got off a single quick shot downhill.

"Couldn't make no deals even if I wanted to," the sheriff growled.

"No," Rudge mused. "I don't fancy you could. But on the other hand, without an accusation and a reasonable hope of conviction you wouldn't waste your time interfering with a citizen's right of innocent passage."

"Don't reckon I would," the sheriff guessed.

"It was a long time ago," Stanley began tentatively. "Hard to say what a man'd look like after all these years."

Rudge laughed. While the Maclendons and sheriff regarded the younger banker with a growingly cynical amusement, Tedrow studied his partner as if he had just discovered symptoms of the pox.

"Don't take it so hard," Rudge consoled.

"You didn't accept this trimmer into partnership," Tedrow said bleakly. "If a banker can't judge character, he's no business in the business."

Rudge gave the disillusioned man a smile. "To the contrary, I believe you were born for it. Once you've divested yourself of that jackal I shall recommend that my co-inheritors put their affairs in your hands."

"Talks just like we was all goin' to be alive tomorrow," the sheriff cackled.

That jackal was not to be put off. Turning to Malcolm and his sister, he offered, "Thirty thousand each."

"Here and now?" Mrs. Lowery asked. "Do you carry that kind of money about with you?"

"He does have it," Tedrow said. "But mostly it's shares in my bank."

"And how sound is that?"

Tedrow shrugged. "Another wild-goose chase like this and you might well ask. But actually, we're in pretty fair shape. And if this opportunist wants out, I'd be delighted to exchange him for the pair of you." He turned and tipped his hat. "Mr. Rudge too."

"I suspect your Mr. Stanley has another proposition for me," Rudge said.

"And what might that be?" Tedrow asked.

"Mr. Stanley is planning on telling the sheriff he was mistaken, that he has never seen or heard of me before—in exchange for my share, of course."

XXI

"This is outrageous!" Mrs. Lowery said. She turned to the sheriff. "And you just sit there and listen while justice is bought and sold?"

"I swore to uphold the law," the sheriff said. "Now Aggie, if you see any law being broken you let me know. And while you're at it, you might tell me how we're gonna fight our way through that trash downhill and git to any courthouse."

"I wonder if they know how many of us there are up here?" Rudge mused.

"But this unspeakable trimmer is perjuring himself!" Mrs. Lowery blazed.

"So's your two-gun *pistolero* friend," the sheriff was beginning when the Springfield went off. Everyone sat quiet for a moment waiting for his ears to stop ringing. While Malcolm reloaded the 50-caliber rifle they began to hear the sounds of confusion down at the bottom of the hill. "Do that a couple more times," the sheriff said, "and them varmints'll learn to keep out of sight."

"How many are left?" Tedrow asked.

"*Son ocho*," the old woman said.

"Eight of them to five of us," the banker mused. "I lived through worse at Chancellorsville."

"Perhaps," Rudge said.

"How do you like *them* apples!" Malcolm snarled.

All hands peered through and around the upended buckboard to see what had upset the boy. Then they were all upset. Another troop of riders was coming upstream from the penny-farthing direction. Rudge remembered that Mrs.

Lowery had said there were other smaller holdings down-stream. Must be close to twenty of the blighters. Every one of them bore some kind of rifle. They also bore large saddle-bags and seemed prepared to stay awhile.

"Wish I could have died in better company," the sheriff growled.

Malcolm turned on the old man. "My sister and I feel the same way!" he snapped. "Now if you can still see past your own belly, how 'bout drawin' a bead on some of them high-graders afore they git dug in?"

Rudge laughed. "Look where they're digging."

"No!" The younger banker went into a howling frenzy. "They can't do that!" he wailed. "That's *mine*."

"Those claim jumpers aren't digging your land," Rudge said. "They're digging Maclendon land. I'd take a dim view of it if the situation weren't so easy to correct."

"What in hell you talking about?" Stanley demanded. "Once they pan it they'll be gone and where does that leave me—us?"

"Sitting pretty, I'd fancy," Rudge said. He turned to the sheriff. "There are no other diggings in these parts, are there?"

"Not in the twenty years I been sheriff."

"They're going to skim the cream and leave us nothing!" Stanley moaned.

"Are they now? And once they've filled their pokes with dust what's the only way out of here? Where do they have to go to spend it, and where are we going to have a sheriff standing by to confiscate every pinch of dust that appears in payment for anything from canned milk to carnal delight?"

"Reckon I could," the sheriff said.

"Reckon you're going to," Malcolm said.

Hope gleamed anew in Stanley's gold-fevered eyes. "I'll give you thirty thousand each," he promised. When neither Malcolm nor his sister seemed interested the apostate banker elaborated. "That's all the cash I've got. Tedrow can tell you that. But I'll give you promissory notes for another ten thousand each, payable a year from today."

"For the whole ranch?" Mrs. Lowery asked.

"He only needs the mineral rights," Rudge said. "Once he's dug the place over for gold those scoundrels will all get out of the way and you can go back to raising sheep again."

"Serve him right if you accepted," Tedrow growled.

The sheriff kept his own counsel.

Mrs. Lowery looked at Rudge. "And you?" she asked.

"What of me?"

"What will become of you if we sign? After all, you own a third."

Downhill there was considerable wrangling going on between the first lot of raiders who had dug in to besiege them *versus* the second lot who were apparently uninterested in who won. Already a couple of them were setting up short sections of sluice box. Another half dozen men were frantically panning up and down the creek.

"Digging up here must've stirred up just enough mud to awaken suspicions," Rudge guessed. "Or perhaps last night's rain washed a bit of color downstream."

Malcolm was aiming at a man whose shovel flashed in a tireless arc as he tossed gravel into a sluice box.

"Don't," Rudge suggested. "Keep out of it and perhaps they'll do in each other instead of us."

"You think it'll work?" Malcolm asked.

"Come nightfall there may be so many people blundering around here that anyone could walk through them without being caught."

"Sixty thousand is all the cash I can raise," Stanley repeated. "Thirty for each of you and I'll give you each a note for ten—make it fifteen thousand."

Tedrow was looking at his partner with undisguised disgust.

"And what deal will you offer me?" Rudge demanded.

"After all, it takes my signature before anything else works."

Down in the creek bottom someone fired a shot. At first Rudge assumed it was another of the high-trajectory lobs they had been trying to drop into the camp up here. Then he saw the sudden separation into sides down below.

But it didn't work out the way they might have hoped. Instead of a war of extermination between newcomers and the besiegers, several placer miners abandoned their pans and tore off downstream again. The remainder joined the pennyfarthings and began throwing up trenchworks from which they could shoot uphill in some comfort.

"'Nother good idea shot to hell," the sheriff said, with a sour grin for Rudge. "Any way you look at it, you're gonna either die here or on the gallows back down in Soda Springs."

"Am I?" Rudge turned to Stanley. "Your offer, sir?"

"Disgusting," Mrs. Lowery sniffed. "Buying and selling men's lives!"

"I'm not dealing in other people's lives, Mrs. Lowery. Only in my own. I can think of no commodity less subject to negotiation."

"I'm not sure I remember your name," Stanley said.

"I'm afraid amnesia is insufficient," Rudge said.

"All right! I never heard of you. I was never anywheres near that corner of Missouri!"

"You're getting warm," Rudge said. "And now how much for the humiliation I've been forced to bear?"

Negotiations broke off at the sound of shattering lumber and an instant later Rudge heard the boom of a buffalo gun. "¡Ay!" the old woman said. A foot-long splinter had gone into one of her bony forearms.

Rudge squinted through the shattered hole in a buckboard bed. Downhill someone had set up a rest and was aiming the heavy buffalo gun again.

It was hopelessly beyond the range of his Colts. He

moved to one side and Malcolm fired the Springfield. An instant later the deep boom of the buffalo gun told them the boy had missed. This time a heavy slug knocked the iron tire off a buckboard wheel. The wheel spun for nearly a minute.

"If I'd known you all were coming," Rudge said to those who groveled about him, "we could have prepared a larger acropolis." He ignored their growls and grumbles as he crawled over them to help Mrs. Lowery with the old woman.

Rosaura endured her wound with the stoicism of a Roman emperor, emitting no single cry of pain after her first startled gasp. Blood gushed as they got the splinter out. Mrs. Lowery exposed an interesting amount of ankle as she tried to rip her petticoat. It was new and refused to rip. Rudge slashed with his clasp knife and they bound the old woman's arm tight enough to stanch the bleeding.

"*Mátalos*," Rosaura recommended, "*pero despacio.*"

"I can't promise to do it slowly," Rudge said, "but I shall most assuredly kill some of them." He turned to Mrs. Lowery who had lost part of her petticoat but none of her appeal. "And how are you this afternoon?" he asked. "You appear somewhat recruited."

She shrugged. Another shot tore into the splintering buckboard and there were assorted cacklings and cluckings while they determined that this time nobody had been hit. "Accept," Rudge murmured.

"I beg your pardon?"

Rudge warned her with a glance. Stanley seemed to be trying to dig his gopherlike way beneath Tedrow who obviously wished he had never met up with this peculiar partner. "It's only mineral rights," Rudge whispered. "Get Tedrow and the sheriff and everyone else to witness the agreement."

"What agreement?"

"The one I'm going to draw up. Complain and play the reluctant virgin if you wish. But *sign it.*"

"Schemin' with her ain't gonna git you out of this," the sheriff warned.

"We were merely deciding whether to toss you or one of your friends to the wolves first," Rudge said. In the glum silence that followed he rummaged through the crates and barrels at one end of their fort until he found paper, pen, and ink.

"Last will and testament?" the sheriff taunted.

Rudge ignored him and continued drawing up an agreement for the sale of mineral rights to the best of his watertight ability. When he had finished writing he handed the document to Mrs. Lowery. Malcolm crowded next to her. "What if Stanley gits killed or just decides not to pay?" he demanded.

Rudge turned to Tedrow. "This document requires your signature too," he said.

"Why?"

"Because a signature is no better than its owner. I suspect you may be afflicted with a terminal case of honesty."

Tedrow laughed. "Wonder if I'll live long enough to find out."

"But if you do, and if Mr. Stanley decides to renege on his agreement, this empowers you to deduct sixty thousand from his shares in your bank and pay the money in equal parts to Malcolm Maclendon and Agnes Lowery. Should there remain the slightest hope of collection, said document also empowers you to squeeze the remainder in promissory notes from Mr. Stanley's no doubt impervious hide."

"Laugh all you want," Stanley said. "Lowery owed me something. This time I'm gonna get big rich."

Rudge glanced at Mrs. Lowery. "Are you sure?" she asked. "Perhaps we should demand a percentage of whatever gold—"

"¡Fírmalo!" Doña Rosaura was an unexpected ally but Rudge was grateful for her support. Malcolm and his sister signed. Stanley signed. The sheriff and Tedrow signed. Then

Rudge spent nearly an hour copying out the document four more times, collecting signatures on each copy. He distributed one each to Malcolm, to Agnes Lowery, to Stanley, and kept the other two for himself.

"Now Mr. Stanley," Rudge said, "you understand that even if you die, this document is binding. Sixty thousand dollars is already legally the property of the Maclendons."

"And the gold's all mine!" Stanley said with a wolfish smile.

"Every last ounce of it," Rudge agreed, "as God and, more importantly, Sheriff Jason, Mr. Tedrow, and myself are witness." The pronouncement was punctuated by another shot from the buffalo gun. Large chunks of sun-hardened wood flew from the buckboard and tore a hole in the tarp they had strung for shade. But nobody was hurt.

"*Mátalos*," Doña Rosaura repeated. "*No importa que sea despacio pero mátalos.*"

Rudge was inclined to agree. It made no difference whether fast or slow. The important thing was to kill those bushwhackers.

Downhill somebody stood to get a better look at the damage and Malcolm's patient posing with the Springfield paid off. He squeezed off a careful shot and had the rifle reloaded before the cloud of black powder smoke cleared. "*Un cabrón menos,*" the boy said with a grin at old Rosaura.

"Malcolm!" Mrs. Lowery snapped. "You will not use language like that!"

"Killin's all right," the boy grumbled, "long's you don't swear."

Only Rudge seemed amused.

He looked at the sun. A while still before dark. He was aching almost as abominably as he had this morning and a day crowded in here under a tarp with all these ill-tempered people had done little to improve his disposition. He elbowed and kneed a space next to the buckboard, acutely conscious that if that buffalo gun scored a direct hit he would no doubt pick up a mortal load of slivers.

Mrs. Lowery stared accusingly as he composed himself for sleep. But Rudge's conscience was clear. He had done everything he could to honor the terms of old Maclendon's will. Now it was in the lap of the gods. He pulled his *sevillano* over his face and silently warned his recording angel not to interrupt the sleep of the just.

And thanks to the miraculous powers of a clear conscience Rudge did doze. When he awakened the sun was down a half hour deeper. With Rosaura out of action from a punctured arm, Mrs. Lowery had concocted a less lethal stew over a carefully concealed fire. She was dishing up. Nobody was paying any attention to the steady whistle of bullets and the occasional thunk as one struck the fort.

XXII

The horses were long gone and, even if the mob downhill did not steal them, it would take days to round them up, hobbles or no. He glanced at Rosaura. The old woman squatted in a corner enduring her bandaged arm with a stoicism learned from a lifetime in this unforgiving country. Rudge thought momentarily of Eusebio up in the mountains. Little hope from up there. Even if he were to abandon his sheep, what difference could one man make against the freebooters downhill who seemed determined to wipe out every last Maclendon?

He turned to the sheriff whose face was nearly as gray as his hair and mustache. "Do those rascals know you're here?" Rudge asked. "After all, you are the law in this county."

The sheriff shrugged. "You want to stand up and tell 'em it's me?"

Considering the steady fire from downhill Rudge thought this tactic unsound. He studied the gray, fatigued man and remembered. "I'm still awaiting your offer."

"A bullet here or a rope in Soda Springs!" Despite age and fatigue there still remained something of the old bucko in Sheriff Jason. "Why should I offer you anything?" he elaborated.

"Because I seem to be for hire," Rudge said. "I might point out that not once have I offered my skills within your jurisdiction. The role was thrust upon me. The Maclendons offered one third of everything, of which by an extant agreement they accept the cash and I the dubious credit of a known scoundrel.

"Said person offers to sell immunity from unspecified events at an unknown time within a nebulous geography. Then we have among us that rarest of all human phenomena: an honest man. Mr. Tedrow has entered into no covenant with me. Doña Rosaura and I have no formal agreement but our aims agree in that we aim at the same target. This leaves only you, Sheriff, with no covenant agreed upon."

"A rope or a bullet," the old man repeated. "I ain't got no use for tinhorns. Should of run you out of town the first time I laid eyes on you."

"Mr. Rudge," the redhead asked, "are we not all in this together?"

"No, Mrs. Lowery, we are not. Your brother has stood off the enemy all day. Has any of our guests fired a single shot in our behalf?" From her face Rudge saw he had not missed anything while he slept. "My only concern," he continued, "was to keep three undecided guns from joining the enemy. But if they wish to remain under our protection, eat our food, drink our water—"

"You'd turn them out?"

"Without their guns and without the slightest hesitation, save perhaps for Mr. Tedrow who seems as much a victim of other people's machinations as am I." He turned back to the sheriff. "You offer no deal for my life. What's the price of yours?"

The gray-faced man managed a grin. "How much you think I got left?"

It was Rudge's turn to laugh. "You and I, thou Antient Mariner, both know that's young man's humbug. You've lived. As each grain of sand drops from your glass the remaining few turn as precious as the yellow dust those swine root for down below."

"All mine!" Stanley cackled. "They're gonna have to turn it all over to me!"

"Just what do you want?" Sheriff Jason demanded.

It was a question that had been bothering Rudge. "I'm not sure," he said. "But I'm entertaining offers."

"Think you stand more chance of getting out of here than any of the rest of us?"

"Like you, Sheriff, I have acquired the habit of living. I claim no lack of momentary doubts and disillusions in the dark of the moon; but I do not expose my head quite so carelessly as does young Malcolm."

The boy ducked down into a less heroic attitude.

"Be danged if I know what'd tempt you even if I could offer it," the sheriff said. "And meanwhile, I don't see you doin' much."

"Good of you to notice that. Just call me Fabius."

"Thought your name was Rudge."

"Fabius Maximus was a Roman," Tedrow explained, "who won most of his battles by waiting with infinite patience for the proper moment."

"Looks like this is gonna be your moment," Malcolm said.

Rudge turned to peer through a crack in the bottom of the buckboard. He glanced at the sun. "Hadn't expected it quite so soon," he murmured.

Downhill the penny-farthings had been busy. Someone had removed the tongue and front axle from the freight wagon Rudge had driven up from Soda Springs. With the aid of dismembered bits of harness they had dangled boards and short pieces of timber skirtlike around the rear of the wagon. This rear-axle-supported breastwork was now being laboriously pushed backward uphill toward the fort.

It was awkward but Rudge had to admire the professional way the penny-farthings had used the materials at hand. It was heavy. They might wear themselves out pushing the device uphill but there was no hurry. There was room behind it for twenty men. Without cannon there was little any marksman could do to dislodge them.

"*Testudo*," Tedrow muttered.

"Except for the wheels," Rudge agreed. "And this one has no roof."

"What in hell you talkin' about now?" the sheriff snarled.

"*Testudo*," Rudge explained, "is turtle in the tongue of the caesars. It refers to the way Romans overlapped shields over their heads while gripping a battering ram."

The sheriff gave a sour cackle. "Well, tinhorn, you got no cannon and no blasting powder. What you gonna do now?"

"I shall take the matter under advisement," Rudge said. He studied the ponderous vehicle that inched uphill. Logic would demand that it be protected by a covering fire but nobody was shooting. Down along the creek several obstinate men still panned and sluiced, paying no attention to the snipping of Norns' shears just out of their range.

"Goddamn high-graders!" Stanley snarled, and fired his first shot—not at the altered freight wagon, but at the placer diggings downstream. Shovels stopped for a moment as miners glanced uphill. Then they went back to their digging.

Rudge wondered at the lack of covering fire. Could they all be coming uphill inside that thing? It would be neat to wipe them out in one fell swoop. But how? He squinted at the makeshift movable fort. It was more solid than the structure he had improvised from buckboards and barrels. It had more men, more guns inside it.

No doubt he could shatter a few ankles and kneecaps once they came close enough. But by then the rifles inside that freight wagon would have splintered his buckboard fort beyond recognition. He wondered what his recording angel would have to say about the situation. But for once his recording angel offered no comment.

Malcolm fired. There was a slight puff of dust where the Springfield slug bounced off weathered timber but the wagon continued its relentless creep uphill.

"Not a true *testudo*," Tedrow muttered.

"Wonder if we have any loose powder about?" Rudge asked.

"¿Pólvora?"

Rudge nodded. No doubt the locals still used muzzle-loading weapons. Shotguns, at least. There was little chance of any great quantity in the Maclendon stores since nobody bothered to blow stumps in this country. He thought wistfully of the cache he had destroyed down by the creek—that had nearly destroyed him.

"Tenga." Doña Rosaura held out a can with her good arm.

Rudge squinted and read, "One pound DuPont choke bore black powder No. 5 grain. Keep in a cool, dry place." He shook the can and sighed. "¿Es todo?"

Doña Rosaura assured him that the half inch of black pepper in the bottom of the can was all that remained of her husband's hunting supplies. Rudge wondered how it could have survived the burnout; then he realized the old man would not have stored anything this dangerous in the same shack where they cooked and slept.

He began poking about the fort searching out whatever could be used to extend this tiny bit of lethal material. First off, he salvaged a half-inch disc of brittle tallow from the gelid remains of the evening mutton stew. He found a fistful of tiny cartridges for the saloon pistol with which Malcolm had saved his life and ended a horse thief's. He ripped handfuls of arid excelsior from the buckboard's ruptured seat cushion. Most of his time though was spent unlaying a length of twine and working black powder into the strands before he twisted it back together in a wrapping of paper and more powder. He was putting the lid back on the can when he had a sudden inspiration. "¿Y el chile?"

Doña Rosaura furnished him with a double handful of the red powder that had done such violence to his digestion. He stirred it thoughtfully into the combustible mass.

"You ain't gonna git no second chance," the sheriff carped.

"Should you persist in airing that news in earshot of the enemy I may decide to shoot you immediately," Rudge said.

"Is there anything I can do?" Mrs. Lowery asked.

"Have the faith that moves mountains. Perhaps you can move this one into the next county."

"My faith is in you, Mr. Rudge. Please do not disappoint me."

"My strength is as the strength of ten," Rudge quoted, "but I most devoutly wish we had a quart of coal oil to complete the offering." He glanced downhill where the freight wagon crept slowly toward them. At the rate they were moving he calculated the penny-farthings would be in range with the last light of day.

"Everyone loaded and ready?" he asked. "If there's to be any last-minute shirking, I'd prefer to settle things now."

"I'm with you," the sheriff said. "But only till they're taken care of."

"Greater love hath no man," Rudge misquoted, "than his own life and chattels."

"When the bullets fly my way I'll not philosophize," Tedrow said. "But I'm truly sorry I ever departed Santa Fe on this wild-goose chase."

"They're stealing my gold!" Stanley snarled, and fired once more at the sluice box that lay beyond any hope of hit. His rifle was one of those small-bore repeaters that had come out since the war. Rudge supposed they would be accurate enough if only their users would aim with the same careful economy that came naturally to the owners of single-shot weapons. Stanley pumped four more shots downstream before turning with a look of manic triumph. He seemed just as happy as if he had hit something.

There was no shot fired in reply. Rudge found this ominous. When the moment of truth came Stanley might be more hindrance than help. The freight wagon had inched another hundred feet uphill.

"Mr. Rudge, have you given any thought to the morrow?"

"A great deal, Mrs. Lowery. But I suspect we talk at cross-purposes."

"Oh?"

"I have prepared a list of questions for my Creator. As I survey the imperfection which Omnipotence created I fear he will not do well under my examination."

"Why," she wondered, "do you go to such lengths to create an appearance of evil?"

"Not I, Mrs. Lowery. I only exist in harmony with the world into which my Creator thrust me."

"God help us all!" Tedrow muttered.

Malcolm's Springfield cracked and there was a howl from inside the converted freight wagon.

"*¡Otro cabrón menos!*" Rosaura cackled.

"I'd rather you didn't do that," Rudge said.

"Why not?" Malcolm demanded.

"Now they'll muddle about for heaven knows how long plugging up whatever opening you discovered."

"So much the better," the boy said.

"Only if you'd prefer them to delay the attack till after dark."

"Ooooooh." It was a long drawn out sound like the wind escaping a smithy's bellows. Malcolm moved away from his splintery loophole and began cleaning his rifle.

But Rudge had been wrong. Instead of discouraging the men in the improvised *testudo*, Malcolm's shot had shown them that they did not have all evening to climb the hill. The freight wagon began moving as fast as twenty-odd men behind it could push.

"For what we are about to receive, may we be truly thankful," Rudge muttered.

Mrs. Lowery sighed. "There are times," she said, "when I almost believe you are an evil man."

Malcolm hastily finished ramming a patch through his rifle and reloaded.

"At the moment I'd settle for convincing those blighters downhill," Rudge growled. He prowled the confines of the fort, doing what he could to make sure each of his ill-assorted army was ready. "Trade the bloody lot of you for half a dozen lads like Malcolm," he groused.

"Can't you talk plain American?" the sheriff growled.

"Also plain Spanish, plain French, and plain Urdu," Rudge snapped. "Give me another year in this benighted country and perhaps I'll master Plains Indian."

"Times I'm goldang ready to believe you *are* a Lime-juicer."

"*Aussi moi,*" Mrs. Lowery said unexpectedly.

Rudge was startled for a moment. He reminded himself that the capable redhead was fluent in English and Spanish. She had been to school in the East. No reason why she shouldn't speak French too.

"I truly suspect you might be the Englishman you call yourself," she continued in that language. "It would be of great comfort to know you had never visited—" She pronounced it Low Runt, which sounds so far from Lawrence that none of the others guessed they were talking about Kansas.

"*Mais il y aura toujours du doute,*" Rudge said with a sad hint of smile.

The hurt was evident as Mrs. Lowery lapsed into English. "Yes," she sighed, "I suppose the doubt would always be there."

"Like the poison in Hamlet's father's ear, corroding all, sowing the seed for new tragedy."

"You have a way with words." Mrs. Lowery could not keep the bitterness from her voice.

"Haven't I though! And strangely enough, I know words that could halt that juggernaut's uphill course, put an end to this ill-conceived affair, and send the penny-farthings skulking back into their fetid holes."

"Sounds jimdandy," the sheriff said. "Why don't you just say 'em and we'll all go home?"

"To be hanged by the neck until dead?"

The sheriff sighed. "Don't look like they's much hope of that. Yon Stanley feller acts like he's been out in the sun too long."

"There also exists another impediment," Rudge said.

"In the name of God, Mr. Rudge, if there's any way to end this without bloodshed—" It was the first emotion Tedrow had displayed.

"Truth often possesses an odd quality: no one wishes to believe it."

"Try us," the sheriff said.

"I suspect you already know. In any event, what you believe is unimportant. It's that carrion below needs convincing."

"Why don't you just tell them?" Malcolm asked.

Rudge sighed. He drew himself to his feet. He was careful not to break cover as he drew a deep breath. "Go home, you ignorant bastards!" he roared. "There ain't no gold. Never was any. Lowery salted it and suckered the lot of you just as he swindled everyone else in his wretched life. Has any one of you panned the slightest hint of color? Now go home and meditate on your sins. The sheriff will call from house to house and arrest the murderers."

He was answered by a moment of shocked silence, then a cackle of laughter. The laughter turned into a fusillade that bounced off the buckboard, splintering the holes larger. Rudge squatted amid flying slivers. "The truth shall make ye free," he said with a sardonic smile.

But the truth had an extraordinary effect on one member of the defending army.

"No!" Stanley shrieked. "It ain't so. It's mine. You highgraders leave my gold alone!" Before anybody could stop him Stanley was out of the enclosure, charging downhill at a dead run, pouring a seemingly endless stream of bullets from his repeating rifle. He was almost on top of the *testudo* before one of the astonished attackers shot him.

There was a long silence inside the fort. "Is anyone else ready for a little truth?" Rudge finally asked.

Nobody answered.

"I'll give it ten minutes," he said.

"Before they attack?"

"Oh damn the attack! Ten minutes maximum before one of you decides I provoked that poor blighter just to destroy the case against me."

"I'm sorry, Mr. Rudge."

"Of course you are."

"But the doubt, as you say, will always be there."

The converted freight wagon was two thirds of the way up the hill by now. Rudge peered between splintered planks and resisted the temptation to act prematurely. Instead, he found a broken cheroot and ignited the longer half. He stood behind the buckboard, concentrating on the approaching fortress. It was well made, with overlapping planks until he could see only the occasional flash of a booted foot. Until they came out of it the penny-farthings were invulnerable. He breathed deeply and tried to wish away the aches and pains that were going to slow him down. His pockets were heavy with extra cartridges. His Colts were polished perfection. He commended his soul to the properly delegated authorities and drew hard on the stump of his cheroot. The sun was half its width above the hills.

"*You didn't have to be so brutal about it.*" It was his recording angel again.

"So how would you have done it?"

There was no reply. He drew deeply on the cheroot. The rolling fort was approaching the brow of the hill, scarcely a hundred feet away. Any minute now they would break into a run. Rudge put out his hand.

"*Aquí está*," Rosaura said, and handed him the near-empty can of black powder and other ingredients.

Rudge drew on the cheroot again and touched his hand-made fuse to its glowing tip. The cord sputtered and burned fitfully, hanging for seconds in one spot, then darting a couple of inches almost instantaneously.

"Throw it!" his army chorused in rising panic. Rudge did not. He posed, holding the canister at arm's length, waiting to see whether the men in the *testudo* would begin their charge before the fuse burned its full length. Finally he could wait no longer. With fire a scarce half inch from the canister he put his all into hurling it.

For a moment Rudge thought he had guessed wrong, that it had gone off in his hand. But the searing pain that enveloped his entire body was only the reaction from straining to hurl a bomb after all the abuse and pounding he had taken in the last few days.

The bomb did ignite in midflight. He had been terribly afraid it would not go off at all. But the packed mass of desiccated wood shavings, mutton tallow, black powder, and saloon-pistol cartridges was hissing like an outraged gander as it plopped inside the roofless breastwork that rolled toward them. The noise increased and greasy black smoke erupted, carrying the searing bouquet of New Mexican chile to eye and throat. There was sudden popping as saloon-pistol ammunition began flying in every indiscriminate direction.

Men came boiling out from behind the freighter wagon. Rudge pulled himself back into reality and drew his Colts. Malcolm had already killed one of them. While Rudge got four penny-farthings, the sheriff and Tedrow each accounted for another. Mrs. Lowery got off a round and handed her rifle back to Rosaura in exchange for a fresh one.

It was pitiful. Rudge killed a man with each shot and when he finished reloading twin Colts some still hovered on the edges of the rolling breastwork, unable to decide between the death that mowed them down from outside or smoking, burning, blinding indiscriminate death from saloon-pistol cartridges and bits of gravel that scattered burning chile and peppered their refuge like a string of Chinese crackers.

Men were crawling downhill—rolling downhill. Rudge began shooting again, making damned sure this time that no penny-farthing life was spared to come back and annoy him. Malcolm was charging outside of their buckboard fortifications. "Come back, damn it!" Rudge roared. But the boy was beyond stopping. Rudge charged after him, Colts roaring as he went around the end of the breastwork.

The burning choking miasma of gunpowder and chile was beyond any of the ingenious devices Rudge had experienced defending the emperor of the Mexicans. He gasped and stepped back for a moment. Behind the fort a balding middle-aged man clawed at his eyes, his mouth open as he knelt to scrabble for a lost rifle. Rudge shot him and put an end to his groveling.

From downhill he heard a confused shouting. As he sensed that there were no more penny-farthings left to kill up here Rudge abruptly understood what the shouting was about. The placer miners were cheering. It puzzled him for a moment, until he understood that in the dim light they couldn't see what had actually happened. After all, with twenty men moving in on the three or four Maclendons, there could be no doubt of how the battle would turn out.

Here and there on the hillside a man still struggled to crawl. With the fighting over Rudge was beginning once more to feel the aches and pains that had plagued him since he had come to this country.

"I believe we can rely on Doña Rosaura for the *tiro de gracia*," he said, and rounded up his comrades in arms. As they marched downhill toward the cheering placer miners nobody remarked that the ancient widow's *tiro de gracia* would no doubt be administered with knife instead of gun.

The claim jumpers were still cheering and waving their hats when Malcolm shot the first one. Rudge remembered what had happened the last time he let one of this lot live. He backed up the boy with his altered Colts. Tedrow and the sheriff stared aghast. "I—I thought you'd warn them and send them away," the banker said.

"Tried that once," Rudge said. "You may have noticed that I'm not walking as straight as I might." He turned to the sheriff. "And before you start any holier-than-thou sermons, I remind you that this is your county. If you'd paid proper attention to your duties, you could have nipped this in the bud."

"I know," the sheriff mumbled. "Lot of good it does me now."

"There's still work for your tin star," Rudge said.

The old man looked bleakly at placer miners scattered like fallen trees, and back to Rudge. There no longer seemed any of the old bucko in him.

"In the Name of the Merciful and the Compassionate, I christen thee Azrael," Rudge said.

"Can't you ever talk straight?" The old man was turning querulous.

Tedrow came to the rescue. "Azrael is the angel of Death." He turned to Rudge. "Women and children?" he asked in anguished tones.

"This is Passover eve," Malcolm explained.

Rudge was not surprised. No Scots boy would be ignorant of the Old Testament.

"We're going to saddle those horses and we're stopping at every spread in this lower valley," Rudge explained. "Any man found home minding his own business will be left there. Those who came to despoil the Maclendons face a simple choice: Leave this country or stay forever."

"You can't do that," the sheriff began.

"You can," Rudge said. "You did it to me. This night you'll ride in front."

It was midmorning before they returned to the hillside fort, red-eyed and bone-weary. And the task had not been as bloody as it could have been. Most of the small spreads downstream had seemed delighted to see them, to learn that the penny-farthing-Oostenveld bullies would no longer claim first fruits in this country.

Even the single slatternly woman in a manless cabin four miles downstream from the penny-farthing spread had seemed to be expecting this kind of news. One of her eyes was purple from some week-old misunderstanding. She accepted Rudge's golden eagle with resignation if not gratitude. On the way home they set fire to the depopulated penny-farthing buildings and pulled gnawed poles from the corral so the horses would not starve.

Mrs. Lowery and old Rosaura had been busy tidying up inside the fort. Outside flies were beginning to swarm around penny-farthing raiders. Rudge accepted coffee and sat in the shade of the tarp. Tedrow and Malcolm were nearly as used-up as Rudge. The gray-haired, gray-mustached, gray-faced sheriff looked like warmed over death. Rudge knew the old man would not be traveling for several days.

"Do you suppose we can go down and start rebuilding now?" Mrs. Lowery asked. In spite of primitive conditions she remained clean and fresh, every lock of abundant red hair in its predestined place. Agnes Lowery was a remarkably attractive woman.

Rudge considered her question. "I'm afraid life seldom offers sure things," he said. "But we've done all that might be done by human hands and will to restore peace in this country. You and your brother are now both considerably richer than before. Will you continue living amid all these ghosts when you could just as easily start anew somewhere else?"

Mrs. Lowery gave the old woman a fleeting glance.

"I understand," Rudge said. "They are your people and without you to hold them together—" He was silent for a moment, then added, "I too was once responsible for a large estate and its people."

"It's they who end up paying for our crimes."

"Crimes?"

"Yes, Mr. Rudge. Lawrence, Kansas, was not the end of it. Now we are all guilty."

"*Sans ombre de douie?*"

"Without a shadow of a doubt," she echoed.

He sighed, trying to evaluate this new viewpoint. There were things to be done—graves to dig. Then they would have to rebuild, round up their scattered herds and herders.

Tedrow and the sheriff sat wooden, not hearing or caring about what had just happened. "Are you quite sure?" Rudge asked.

"We must all stop somewhere, Mr. Rudge."

It was tempting. Rudge could not remember when he had been so tired, so in need of a quiet spot. "'Spose I could stick around long enough to help you get things back on rails again," he said.

Mrs. Lowery smiled a self-contained and secret Scots smile.

Rudge glanced around and saw that Malcolm was quietly weeping. He supposed it was a good sign.